Obuseencentfinitus

Obits Seen for Centuries
if Not for an Infinity

By

Emma L Reid

MAPLE
PUBLISHERS

Obuseencentfinitus

Author: Emma L Reid

Copyright © Emma L Reid (2025)

The right of Emma L Reid to be identified as author of this work has been asserted by the author in accordance with section 77 and 78 of the Copyright, Designs and Patents Act 1988.

First Published in 2025

ISBN 978-1-83538-371-1 (Paperback)
978-1-83538-585-2 (Hardback)
978-1-83538-372-8 (E-Book)

Cover Design and Book Layout by:
White Magic Studios
www.whitemagicstudios.co.uk

Published by:
Maple Publishers
Fairbourne Drive, Atterbury,
Milton Keynes,
MK10 9RG, UK
www.maplepublishers.com

A CIP catalogue record for this title is available from the British Library.

A Tiny Info/Synopsis Entry... (Possibly Summary)

Just before their exile to 'O' (said Dime) swore of a vengeance towards 'Sierephiar' and that they would see the fall of their kind and destroy the unity of 'The Grid'.

When 'She' realises whose voice she heard on 'Sierephiar' her 'Dime' target becomes clear and her missions - 'Mind-Ins' to her, become more vivid how she should execute them.

Introduction

'Inner-Site' Intro...

'Mind-In' visions give an abundance of insightful information, wisdom, steeped deep in knowledge and ways of Dimensions, spanning billions of years of techniques mastered for syphering vital mind intelligence, useful for the continuation of 'all species' within the 'Minlactic' cluster.

Somewhere along the time path of this cluster system, a break within their connection with one another, set a severing that would divide their trust of each other, and a paranoia, set deep within each Dimension - this saw the foundations of a united nation of selected Dimensions.

This was the world of...

'The Grid'

CONTENTS

Chapter In...

"You've got that same look on your face."

The look to him, was one that seemed to have visualised this scene a thousand times played over, remembering only of its panic created of a known destruction seconds away from its relived, repeated agony, of witnessing the wipe out of their species.

As the ground beneath them split and that growling, raucous rumble, ripped through their land, she answered in that snapped to reality once again tone ...

"I know?"

She answers, wondering why? ...

Panic, all again, repeated terrorising fear, his face, every time a picture she seemed to only indulge of its desperation to run, save itself, save her and her people, all in unison, scatter and total chaos breaking out, all this also, her mind already knew, but repeats and the experience is as though it is the first every time.

Why? ...

Why does she not remember in time, why not a little more time, so she can save them...

Save 'her'.

Why does her mind never connect in time?

Again, she is too late... Again 'She' is too late...

"Seenhigh-Sypher 221811, where were you located on The Grid, when the instructions for the jump were given?"

The atmosphere within the court, though tense, was of a verdict, already predicted, the people were already decided.

These questions from the Orbit Board were always the same, someone needed to fit the responsibility bill, someone needed to realistically be believable for the masses to accept that a certified one must be the one that would orbit to 'O'. Sheer determination enveloped her body. 'She' would convince them. 'She' - 221811 would always be, always knew... *it had to be her.*

The people would start ...

"221811 221811 221811." The whispers would start sparingly, then as they grew stronger and more collectively among almost the whole yard...

"Seenhigh-Sypher 221811... You will orbit to 'O' this time."

Yet again, she had won the vote of the masses.

"I will not fail."

Complete roar ripped through the crowd.

"Be fearful," she thought.

" 'O' be very fearful of me."

Slipping quietly away from the crowds, she would always retreat to her place of sanctuary, the only place her mind could sypher out, be un-syphered, rest, find peace.

She walked calm, undisturbed, floating almost, but something was different, not different imposing or threatening, but unusually... different.

The pebbles felt peculiar this time, she couldn't tell, they seemed to shine more to the west.

She was looking into things too much, she was feeling an un-explainable pressure, not uncomfortable though, thinking to herself - only a few more chances, she only had a few more chances. Yes, the Dimension Grid would still exist...

She still could not understand why she was feeling this panic. Why...?

"Still thinking one step ahead of time?"

Ripped suddenly from her trail of thought, almost as if her mind became panicked from being attacked by another intrusive mind invading hers, forgetting what she was fixated on, she looked to see who was unexpectedly in her company.

'She' was not expecting anyone.

'He' was so mystifying, it seemed as though she had known him forever. She did not understand how she found such comfort within his presence. Why would she? She did not know him.

Instantly, she grew a kind of comfort with their connection, almost as though his presence brought her calm, and as long as he was there she somehow believed that within this encounter, an immediate sentiment secured her. There was always a chance, she would come home.

One: 1 Chapter In

"She has been here before; I recognise her dimension skin."

"How can you be so sure, Aliave?"

Aliave was always suspicious, but this particular moment, his unease was more intensely noticeable.

"Genvia, if you do not intercept her coming to this, our Dimension, I feel we will be regretful of this conversation for eternity and our species' chances of surviving The Grid will slim with knowledge becoming less vivid and grey in shade not knowing how to react or revive us!"

Genvia 'felt' from him on this specific occasion, his tension. She answered as she would always.

"Aliave, I have always 'reacted' as you so put it, with Sierephian Tribe instinct, honestly and fair to 'all' Grid Dimensions. This is the only way I know how to react. If that is not enough to keep our kind within the Grid, then Aliave, I'm afraid you'll have to accept that our kind... are not supposed to remain in it."

Aliave, though frustrated with the response, pushed with his next question all the same, also knowing not to push too temptingly, of overstepping respectful boundaries.

"Are you Genvia, going to greet her at the jump, when she lightens in?"

Aliave was always one to test boundaries, I might add, reader, but 'this' he really edged, with testing the waters and knowing Genvia would never agree to meet jumps to their Dimension, would she? Or should she ever answer differently...

Genvia knew this, answering Aliave the way 'she' knew would halve his tormented stance, and hopefully lessening the chance of him having a (already) staunch approach towards their unexpected guest.

"No Aliave, I'm appointing you to welcome her, I feel your reaction will best inform her of her decision of which task or path she must choose. I have spoken, you must observe how you'll follow with your mind's command."

Aliave had an instant satisfactory ease within him, answering Genvia swiftly, "I will do my best." With immediate reaction, he set to command his preferred action towards their new guest.

Aliave sat focused towards his troops, who were waiting, ready for order.

Syphering to his main mind-in soldier.

"Locline, where does it show she will lighten?"

"In the pitch, Aliave."

Locline, always ready, and always efficient.

"Already, I feel her coming is of an anguish for Sierephiar," Aliave stated.

Locline became unsettled very quickly, as he could feel the tension from Aliave and through past experience with Aliave, unsettled, meant complex work, and meant 'all' had to scrutinise decisions harder and with tunnel focal mind-in concentration, 'victory-must' mindsets, than usual.

"What did Genvia say?"

Locline pressed, hoping Aliave would give an answer, with an answer within it, Genvia may have said, helping them with solving their newfound problem.

"Never enough to guide us with sure knowledge that we will triumph,"

Aliave so obviously answered.

Locline was disappointed, but not surprised at all... still... now was not the time for individual doubt, all heads or minds needed to be combined, firm, no space for any weakness.

"Where would you like me to highlight you to, Aliave?"

"The upper region of the pitch Locline, there I will be able to second sight her Dimension. If her visit is not fully for a just cause, at least The Grid will be able to trace her jumps and where she has previously lightened, then, they can stop her, if she is a threat to our or any other Dimensions."

Sierephiar, a place protected within a sacred firmament, peaceful in its veneration of continuous vicegerent devotions towards its deep beliefs of a supreme energy, coating and respirating its fields with an abundance of neutralisation.

Jadelain was indulgently encapsulated by it all.

An overwhelming sense of calm enveloped her person, her persona changed, she was confused - was she here to wipe or keep this Dimension? She felt peace here, her mind questioned, rapidly, intensely...

"I can't be here to wipe?... they can't be a threat to our kind?... The Board, they've got this wrong, this species is too peaceful, I must relay my mind's findings-in-thought, I need to warn them immediately of my change in feeling... how was this not read right before?"

Syphering back to her comrade, Jadelain minded-in her position, and that she was readily set for lightening.

"Seenhigh-Sypher 221811 about to lighten."

"221811, we've highlighted you to the Pitch region ...221811, is something wrong, you're not responding?"

Doubt (221910) already began to feel.

Jadelain's (221811) mind rapidly flittered, she could not settle.

"221910, I don't think The Board have got this right, I feel strongly about this one."

"221811, you say this about most jumps, and you're always wrong. Don't change things now, we're so close to remaining on The Grid... permanently...221811? 221811?!" ...

A pause, though slight, but seeming a lifetime for 221910, waiting for 221811 to answer.

"Not this time," 221910 threatened inside.

'221811' she thought. Needed and was an absolute 'must' that she get 'this' particular mission right.

"221910, I'm ready to lighten."

A direct answer.

"Good," 221910 replied, sighing with relief.

All 221910 need do within this mission, was make sure direct orders were received and a direct understood response followed from whoever was appointed for the mission, then she was no longer responsible, out of the loop, and the appointee immediately became sole and solo commander of the execution of the assignment.

"... please 221811, please avoid our wipe ..."

Jadelain (221811) gave an evasive but direct response to 221910.

"I can only do my best to keep us safe, 221910 and my best is always based on my instinct."

This was enough for 221910 and she made a point of pressing Jadelain no further, she had her direct answer. Nothing, nor no one would benefit so far into the mission, if she was to question Jadelain more and now Jadelain was no longer her friend. She was Seenhigh-Sypher 221811, higher ranking than 221910 and therefore it would be inappropriate of her to question a senior's decision.

And this suited her...just fine.

Back, in another part of Sierephiar, Aliave readied himself to meet their unexpected guest (and frankly for him, unwanted).

"Locline, do we have her lightening secured?"

"Yes, Aliave. Aliave, I must warn you; we cannot identify her."

Aliave's suspicions grew stronger, but with a slight edge of smug, feeling he already had the upper hand, this having a better, more calming, more victorious effect among the troops, just the moral boost they needed.

"That Locline, is all the justification I need... I'm ready to highlight."

"Shall I inform The Grid?"

Locline questioned, panicking.

"No need, Locline, she has just given us all the reason to eliminate her mind, I'll take over fully with this encounter... highlight me closer, the quicker we deal with this, the better for all."

Though Locline 'still' was unsure of this command, the confidence within Aliave eased his uncomfortableness slightly.

"As your mind commands Aliave... Our thoughts are all with your instinct, remember Aliave... trust your intuition," Locline desperately insisted.

"As always Locline, as always ..." Aliave directly reassured.

As Jadelain faded through with her lightening to The Pitch, the cutting calm made her feel an unease, then she noticed? ...

"221910, I'm here, funny, no one is here to observe me... are you sure you gave our Dimension's cordial, general intent?"

221910 quickly answered Jadelain, with a direct and the answer she was commanded to give her, from their Board of Officials.

"221811, the affirmed conscious intent was given ..."
...

221910 knew she could not buckle, as it was common ground on their Dimension that not all information given to all of them was the same among their groups, but it was known, in sync, by them 'all' that no matter what, you 'all' had a duty to deliver whatever command, even if that meant ...

She proceeded with her answer to Jadelain, in a more benevolent tone.

"221811, you're on your own now, as you always know, we cannot protect your mind, all the memories we have selected for you, are now in-fixed, how you choose to select or piece them together for this mission, is entirely your or your mind's better choice."

She continued, hoping Jadelain could hear in her the willing to get this right, and ... to ...just come home.

221910 continued ...

"I've trusted and believed every time you've set out on your tasks, that you'll listen to your deep inner intuition… every time, you've proven, you do… do what you always do, 221811, do what we expect of you… trust your instinct, we're counting on it …"

Jadelain knew, could hear the dependency 221910 had on her (Jadelain's) 'specific' responsibility, not only of her mission, but more importantly… that …

That 'her' friend return safe and sound.

"Ok Jadelain," she thought to herself.

"You are no longer Seenhigh-Sypher 221811, you are seemingly far away from home to channel into your inseminated mind's projections now, it could cost you and your kind being wiped… instinct Jadelain, instinct …"

The Pitch.

It did not feel like any place within a Dimension she had ever been before, its calm and peaceful atmosphere was just too diluted to encourage an influential unease, this seemed deluding, confusing almost…

Why?… Why was she sent here? Maybe there was an undertone, an underlying, destructive element within it, maybe that was it, it was a complete delusion. This place, she was beginning to think, was the reason - Dimensions were being wiped, it was a distraction, a diversion, created to deceive all Species, all Dimensions… The Grid.

She trekked towards, what she thought she could make out, was a path. Everything here, the air, the trees, even the ground seemed to persuade you to walk an already mapped out voyage.

She still could not reassure herself she was meant to carry out this mission for a later outcome for this kind, all the validations, the jump without any interference, all the knowledge gained and received by her to guide her through, was completed, no variance. The land itself on this Dimension willingly guided her on, but still, her doubts were not eased, she was not satisfied with her feelings, her intuition wasn't settling within her...

Something was wrong, terribly wrong, and for the first time, she could not channel into what was troubling her.

Yet, for some reason, her mind told her to push on, somehow convincing her, against all these odds... this was the path to lead.

Her mind sensed a presence of clustered thoughts, there were many, much more than what would usually greet her ... why had so many come to observe her, why did this feel like it would be instant interrogation of her mind?...

Suddenly realising, Jadelain thought, "This was not a welcoming to this Dimension, this was an army, she had been double played."

She needed to lock in and protect the thought variations that had been inseminated in her mind, if this was not telepathically exchanged correctly with or received in the format visual, she had imprinted in her mind, she would run the risk of exposing crucial visions that would certainly crush, wiping her, and most definitely other Dimensions linked to her and her own kind.

The panic encompassed her whole person, she hadn't even had time to recap the placements of these inseminations, she hadn't memorised the mental visions of each thought, each memory. She would not be able to pick them out, realistically, believably. She would stumble, that fraction of a second, would be obvious, they would suspect instantly...

"What should I do?! What should I do?!"

Her thoughts rapidly juddered...

Then suddenly, as though, everyone or thing present, was quietened, a peaceful silence covered her whole body, like a glistening film of harmonious notes, a voice...

"Calm Jadelain, you will complete your task, it is time, calm your thoughts, let it come naturally."

Looking intensely around her 'who was the voice'? Despairing, she questioned in her mind.

Then suddenly she noticed, her mind doing something she had never done before, at a speed she never knew could be reached. Her mind began to focus only on the thought of who was most relevant to her next move, her thought process only chose the mind opposite to her, that was most definitely going to determine a positive, the better outcome for her, for her kind.

This process, she, her mind, was not, had never used.

Countless times in the past, she would have had several mental options to choose from, hoping always to choose the right one. Now her mind was mapping it out for her, the thought visions were so vivid, she could almost smell the atmosphere within them.

There, there was her target… Aliave Alyious.

If his death meant the death of all Sierephians, then so be it.

Her mission had become clear, she was no longer undecided.

Locking her mind into her target, the tone of her mental voice channelling to Aliave was coarse, this causing Aliave to mind back to her an answer with slight *mocking,* but a defensive mental tone also.

"You say my name as if you knew of me knowing you were coming… Jadelain,

Why?"

Aliave looked puzzled and confused, yet still he maintained a staunch stance, this aggravated Jadelain and Aliave could see that.

He knew this was the chance to ease her doubts, but instead persisted to torment her discomfort, after all, as far as he was concerned, she had no official right to be in Sierephiar and the Sierephian kind hadn't invited *her.*

"I feel, somehow, *I did* already know of 'your' coming?"

Aliave continued *'still'* with a mental taunting mind-in tone.

Jadelain abruptly, but this time with a more disciplined, concentrated, firm stance, minded back. "Why wouldn't you... Aliave... after all you have my assigned intentions, do you not?"

Aliave answered with what would seem to be, reader, a bluffed response.

"Well of course, I just wanted to be sure it was truly you, with all that has been occurring within the Grid... no one wants to be wiped??" ...

"Why did he mention that?" ...

Deep within her mind, Jadelain began to question.

She knew she mustn't allow her memory to be read wrong, she must limit her thought process, and with deep disappointment, she thought.

"Such a peaceful Dimension, what a disguise, they had been able to deceive The Grid...They would not deceive her."

Questioning Aliave further, she asked, "How did your Dimension come to be so calm, so Intune, almost as though you have eliminated doubt and indifferent thinking?"

"You say this like you feel this is a new requirement. Sierephians and the land of our Dimension have practised this from a time, able to remember, no other way was ever known."

Aliave answered, almost shocked she should ask such a question, ignorance was one thing to him, but common knowledge, even he felt surprised, she did not know of their Dimension's ancient practices and steeped, almost embedded ways of the Sierephian lands, his dislike for her, fed his 'now' compulsion or desire to eliminate her mind even more.

Jadelain then answered, as if to completely dismiss Aliave's sense of importance and hierarchy over her.

"Quite convenient for the containment of visiting minds like my own."

And Aliave with his blatant arrogance, spat back.

"Yes Jadelain, much needed, especially for visits such as yours."

"Oh, and what of my special visit?"

"Well, Jadelain… knowing of your role, as to why you generally visit Dimensions, lands like ours… remind me, I'm led to believe you find this place, what was it…peaceful??"

Aliave had struck a nerve, how did he? …

"Yes, I genuinely do …"

Jadelain was genuinely confused, the land was so peaceful, but she knew, she must keep her head.

She was surprised of his knowing of her initial inner concern of their Dimension before her lightening there…

"And now," she exclaimed, "now I understand why you must all think in unison."

A counter defence answer.

"Oh, *and why is that?*"

Aliave beckoned for her to continue, as he could not see why *this* was such a problem for her.

Jadelain proceeded to explain her reasoning.

"Because any doubt amongst you all, would create an illusion of other."

"An illusion of other? Jadelain!"

Now Aliave was genuinely confused.

"The truth Aliave ..."

The first thought insemination revealed itself to her, it was of a Dimension she was sent to jump to, she was asking for aid from them, to secure her Dimension's involvement in honouring a Species with their introduction to The Grid.

Aliave's confusion grew stronger, he asked her, "Why do you feel Jadelain, you must mind-in this particular memory, do you feel I would not trust your kind?"

"Quite the opposite, in fact Aliave," Jadelain prompted.

She continued ...

"I'm showing you this because as you can see, the Species in question, were from modest beginnings. Remember, they had no intention of joining the combined league of nations, like yourselves, they believed only in peace. With them joining the nation, they were able to convince other Dimensions, that a one-united front was all that was needed to stop 'O' from destroying us all."

"I don't understand Jadelain, we are already a part of The Grid?" Aliave desperately answered.

At that moment, seconds between, two memories sped through Jadelain's mind, so fast she could hardly visualise them, piece them together, in fact, all this also before Aliave could finish his sentence.

The fear and dread she felt instantly from them.

They were both so blurred, vague, little time to make sense of them.

The first of a land, a Dimension wiped, this was wrong, why was this linked to Sierephiar, what did they do?!

Then of... Obuseencentfinitus... the connection. She knew she only orbited to such a place when more in depth, permanent actions were required. She had no time to link the exact connection, Aliave would read her mind, he would discover she knew...

"What is this memory, Jadelain, you show me of 'O'?"

"Why Aliave?... do you wish to send your Seenhigh-Sypherers to The Grid? What information do you have? Why to 'O'? Who do you want wiped?"

With what Aliave could see with this mind-in from Jadelain, instinct kicked in ...

"Clever Jadelain, clever girl, I don't know how you extracted that memory, so deep down hidden in my mind, but I can assure you now, you will not leave Sierephiar undiscovered, The Grid will be informed of your conduct... detain her! ..."

Aliave's troops hastened towards her, but feeling a surge, a force, she could not be eliminated, a greater power, stronger than the land of Sierephiar itself, engulfed them.

"Silly Aliave, you failed to inquire about what Seenhigh-Sypherer was visiting... I have already informed them of your activity, my mind-ins are known for my ability to relay information simultaneously whilst interrogating my target... such a shame for Sierephiar, what was it... peaceful... goodbye Aliave ..."

Within an instant, she channelled through to her home Dimension...

"Seenhigh-Sypher 221811 ready to jump home... Dimension Sierephiar... wiped from Grid ..."

She could not help, going over and over, in her mind, the last inseminated memory given to her, so vague, but enough to convince The Grid for the wipe of Sierephiar.

Why did Aliave want them wiped?... What did they do?...

The vision of the conversation she had with him. Him and his kinds' contact with 'O'.

No, (she continuously deliberated in her mind) she could not make out what was being said, but The Grid understood her stricken time with dealing with Aliave, the wipe and relaying the appropriate information, to gain the ok from their selves to go ahead with the wipe.

She did not do what 221910 had asked...

She did not go with her instinct.

Home.

Tired and with a hunger so overpowering in her belly, Jadelain was glad to be home, the greets back were the best, the only thing to look forward to on her Dimension and although the pleasantness of the sensation of feeling welcomed back did only last moments, it was enough of an illusion to always keep you coming back; after all, no other Dimension wanted you.

Jadelain sat, feasting with her only friend, longing to address her by name, so to make their conversation all that more personal, but dent she would, no *'real'* relationships were allowed here.

Her colleague quizzed her.

"Seenhigh-Sypher 221811, you have managed to intrigue my view of you again, you have completely thrown my knowing of your method within your movements."

"221910, I hope you still remain confident with my decisions?"

"I only hope 221811, they are in favour 'still' of our Dimension and I hope… you are still instinctive to the best ability, best outcome, for us all."

This impersonal approach was always the nature of their conversations, this was …

Home.

Two: 2 Chapters In

Back...

Lying, almost motionless, body adjusting from a mission, seeing her discovering, forced learning, and instantly practising, with unknowing, sheer chance-taking, having to trust, unwillingly, no choice given, of a technique, a method, never used, had no knowledge she could.

Yet her intuition, her highest sense of mental instinct she knew, had, what seemed to her, a pre-built-in memory, imprint of this, giving her direct faith to use this ability and as she did, it was as if she had always practised it-'it' was always there and she could neither remember where it came from, the beginnings, nor remember the continuation, bringing to the forefront of her mind, the right way, with no hesitation, to use it...

Confidently... effortlessly.

Her mind deepened into memories of the past, early encounters she was remembering, with 'others', different kinds, other Dimensions.

Trying to piece together, the connections, why?

What were the reasons The Grid was failing, what or who was causing the breakdown between different

Dimensions, why was trust, credence with one another weakening?

We, 'all', she continued in her mind, within The Grid, simply, were losing faith in one another... we were beginning to be, it seemed, divided.

Who or what was causing the divide, needed to be discovered and fast, her mind was so troubled and conflicted, this also causing her frustration, and with the desperation for her mind to find the answers, the answer was becoming harder to figure out, almost as though, the more she thought, the more it slipped away from her.

Deeper into mind oblivion she went, fading, fading into a past memory ...

Trasuprimatul and its kind, Trasuprimordials, had always, it seemed to her, had an unquestionable (for neither them or any passing its land) calm, warm, welcoming.

There was no fear felt by you, from them, ever betraying your trust in them and your safety (whilst residing there) becoming endangered.

The reminiscence of being in over there, the first few times, her mind deepened in...

Their gerontocracy order, though, subtly intimidated you, but only so to keep you within the lines of their governing. You were already prepared to cooperate within their order, as your mind had persuaded you, had given you solace, their way, you could adopt, adapt to your own practices and principles.

Their Dimension was ancient, and you could see this, the cobbled, time beaten old stone, an industrialised megalopolis.

Steeped in historical Mind-Ins, these being shared only amongst the wiser, higher-powered, higher cerebral intelligent, intellectual rulers.

Drifting deeper still, she ascended to a distinctive, specific, detailed visit.

Her mind, within this moment, chose to fixate upon a conversation whilst there, glancing into the visual window of this, recalling and remembering, she dazed reflecting upon the memory whilst there, of this, jumping straight to the conversation, that whole moment, she could remember she had experienced ...

"How did it come to be so complicated? It's as though, 'all' our Dimension's teachings, the whole collective of us within The Grid, are fracturing, we're losing our way, our own beliefs in systems spanning back to the beginnings, for most our worlds, our initial laws, practices, which were never changed, could never be changed...

"These systems see us, secured us, stood us firm through 'all' our challenges, where 'all' (especially) on The Grid, see great benefit, success, and now... now, none feel assured, not even to speak with confidence, of their own or any other kind."

"Jadelain, come now, you are always so quick to accept the worst, inviting the bleak into the more vulnerable, sensitive inner channels of your mind. Try... please try, Jadelain.

"You know, one day young lady, you will give in to seeing, and glimpse what your mind is so desperately striving to reveal to you... Stop fighting your mind, child."

"I fear these visions so greatly," thought Modyous. "When they surface, an overwhelming intrusion takes place in my mind, and I panic.

"Then the process begins again, but not all is clear, there are holes, fundamental holes, and that is where the panic stems from, I feel my mind's anxiety, its desperation, trying to withhold, reveal to me, this vital information.

"But as I slowly come round to full consciousness, they fade and for a brief moment, I remember, what seems to me, a kind of repeated visit to these visions, then... gone, they fade out?"

Modyous.

Jadelain was remembering Modyous, no she had not forgotten him, but as our minds do, certain memories get pushed back and when your brain or mind needs aid of them again, almost as though it were yesterday, there, there they are, the use for them comes, finally.

Jadelain's mind focused in more vividly to this memory, feeling even the smell of the air of that moment, this memory, the importance of its use for her now, was now ready to be selected, channelling more into it clearly, she could feel, hear the conversations, the events of that moment, word for word, and every actioned final outcome.

Hearing Modyous as if he were speaking to her now, remembering what he said to her then ...

"Jadelain, do you remember much of your home Dimension, your origins?...I ask you this as your kind, although unwilling to join allegiance with The Grid, gave you to the lands of Zardinelle.

"They believed Jadelain, that the creation of The Grid enhanced a multiple of outcomes, within all Dimensions, most of these being of the worst, hence their adamant decline to The Dimension Grid's proposed offer for them to join..."

Modyous continued ...

"It has never been fully clear, to 'our' Dimension especially, why the handing over of you was made. It has had mixed emotions from 'all' within The Grid ever since... thoughts have seen many deliberating, endlessly, were you a sacrifice??

"I myself, if I must admit, have at times, been divided by the sheer presence of you, yet, when you leave, I pray deep mind-ins of a despairing scale, hoping desperately for your survival."

Jadelain, surprisingly remembered, within this part of the conversation, the puzzling unease Modyous felt, to continue with her, almost as though he did not feel confident enough to carry on with what he was about to put forward to her. This was unusual for her as

Modyous was 'always' confident with his interactions with anyone, with Jadelain herself.

She could hear him again in her mind, say to her …

"Jadelain, I have wanted to try a technique with you, I know it is possibly risky and may change the outcome for us 'all' but, I feel strongly, your visit, this time around, is the time to attempt. My intuition here today, strongly, tells me so."

Jadelain remembered her reply and her confusion at the time.

"But Modyous, I have never before felt doubt with you, and I feel none now. I am more than willing to attempt this method; I want no more than the other minds on The Grid to have peace, comfort."

Modyous swiftly continued.

"That statement Jadelain, I feel strongly, believe incessantly, will soon no longer be, just a notion, it will be truth, continuously, forever, for all on The Grid, and all Dimensions, everywhere. Come Jadelain, let's walk."

"Where to?"

"To the only one of our kind, a master in this technique, that can wield, with truly little disturbance of your other thoughts, the source of these visions… Mimuluan."

Jadelain was surprised (back then), she had replied, "But Modyous, she has very little tolerance for me as it is."

"Yes, you're right… and that is the reason she relentlessly pounds my mental tolerance, to intolerance and near, sheer instability, insisting I bring you to her."

"Mimuluan insists on seeing me??!" Jadelain blurted.

Modyous subtly laughed to himself, replying to her, "Jadelain, she has insisted ever since your first jump here. Her cold shoulder towards you has only been an indirect frustration with me."

He insisted, attempting to enhance Jadelain's confidence in what he was saying, then adding,

"I have only now felt you were ready."

"You see Jadelain, you must understand, Trasuprimordials are not known for rash thinking, and 'I' for one, most certainly will not be starting now.

"The rendition of this, must, and can, only be of a successful revelation, and even with that statement I have just made, I still feel no guarantee, nor a 100% sentiment within it, I am completely throwing caution to the wind, and as you already know of me, it is not something I do Jadelain. We, I, simply cannot afford to take these risks …

"And yet …Here I am 'still' continuing, only going on 'my' gut instinct, and I still do not have a full mind-in confirmation, solid enough to be fully sure."

Jadelain looked on in despair, she could see the desperation in Modyous, but that also, his hands *were* tied, that he had absolutely no choice to do other things, as if he had exhausted all other options, asking him ...

"Then why Modyous, are we attempting this?"

Modyous glanced at Jadelain, looking deep within her, knowing to himself even with all his doubts, this really was the option he must go for, he answered her with this expressed upon his face, answering directly to her mind, so as to make sure she understood, this *'must'* be done.

"Because Jadelain, Mimuluan has recently stressed to me that we are running out of time and the only piece, part of information that convinced me of her desperation, was of your coming."

Jadelain's confusion continued, becoming frustratingly questionable in her mind of the outrageous chance Modyous was making her understand he was about to take. She questioned him further, with a puzzling anguish on her face, for what could be so daringly risk taking, worth losing all the merits he and his kind had accumulated with The Grid, and even more so ... doing this with her involvement.

Further, Jadelain stated ...

"But you always know of my coming."

Then Modyous began to explain.

"Yes Jadelain, you're right, we do, but you know also how mind-ins work, you have to choose, using sheer intuition, the right vision."

He went on ...

"Mimuluan's technique is far more advanced, she is able to select visions, only useful for that given moment. Her visions have been dominated lately only of the future."

This did not make sense to Jadelain, it was unclear what Modyous was trying to say, she asked further …

"Why are you telling me this?"

Modyous calmly answered, "Because Jadelain, her future visions were linked to another significant day, and I feel that day is today" …

Suddenly, another familiar voice, Jadelain heard.

"Jadelain, finally, a mind-in by myself, that sees the right instinctive persuasion of Modyous's mind."

Jadelain's surprise at who had just joined her and Modyous' company, was felt 'heard in her voice'. She answered, almost excitingly, but with slight doubt in her body, for still she did not know what was being asked of her and why both such parties were asking of her 'specifically' with a slight hysterical tone to her mind-in, answering …

"Mimuluan, I had no idea, no sixth intuition, you were pursuing my attention."

Modyous took it upon himself to answer Jadelain first, with her flustered surprise of Mimuluan joining them suddenly, and trying to answer Jadelain back with a more calming tone, he knew desperately that Jadelain needed to be tranquil for what was about to be put to her.

He attempted to soothe her uneased confusion with the whole engagement, stating …

"That's right Jadelain, every time Mimuluan would tell me of these visions and of the ones specific to any jumps here from you, I instinctively knew, that there could be no link, no pre-sight, by you, connecting to her vision at the time, the right jump. I felt strongly that you could not, must not, see any mind-ins or any specific reasons to be here.

"You needed to be completely mutual, a visit purely based upon amicable terms.

Mimuluan had that vision…

And here you stand."

Jadelain answered this statement the only way 'any' could answer it, as 'still' she had no further understanding of what was happening and happening specifically with her.

She continued to quiz, both Modyous, and well … Mimuluan also?

"So, all the jumps I made here, Modyous, me being lightened here sometimes by my own Dimension, you have been waiting for the right initiation?"

Modyous knew he must answer her directly to what he could make her understand for that moment, for he knew, reader, if he digressed with any information or Jadelain had any doubt, it would jeopardise his and Mimuluan's quest or desire for her, he desperately needed to keep her on board, on side. They just could not afford to lose her confidence, her trust, or her companionship now.

He quickly continued …

"Yes Jadelain, and every time my senses told me otherwise, I painstakingly withdraw, especially your inner assumptions of Mimuluan, your instincts with her were growing stronger, making it harder for me to pick the right moment to initiate with you."

Jadelain was perplexed by this comment, stating to Modyous,

"But Modyous, I still had my assumptions of Mimuluan today."

Mimuluan stepped in.

"Yes, Jadelain, you did, but I asked Modyous to propose 'you' seeing me, at a time, that I did not choose, nor tell him when and where I see my vision."

This was all very confusing for Jadelain, but she was intrigued now, so she pressed Mimuluan further.

"Your vision of what, Mimuluan?" Jadelain asked stirringly.

At that moment, Mimuluan, recited the complete answer given by Jadelain to Modyous after his proposal to the technique…

"This was what you answered to Modyous, Jadelain; Modyous, I have never before felt doubt with you, and I feel none, now. I am more than willing to attempt this method; I want no more than the other minds on The Grid to have peace, comfort."

Jadelain was taken back by this but was also intimidatingly impressed, as usually whenever another syphered into any mind-ins she was having with others, she, her confidence in her ability to pick up on it, was strong, yet she did not detect Mimuluan syphering her and Modyous' meeting, this intrigued her, for how was Mimuluan able to do this??!

Mimuluan continued …

"I reassured him, this would be your answer, with exact dialogue from you. When he would feel the right time to ask, with his ever-growing complication of your intuition growing stronger of me, this was the only way I could convince him, this was the right time. It had to be his choice, but you needed to answer this way."

Jadelain began to settle with this sentiment.

She had another question for Mimuluan.

"Mimuluan, please, I'm curious to know what these visions entailed for me?"

Mimuluan's answer puzzled Jadelain.

"Jadelain, I cannot explain or make you understand verbally. I must use dialogue that can only involve a mental vision. You see, Mind-ins connect to multiple outcomes." To Jadelain what Mimuluan was explaining was simple Mind-ins. She stated this …

"So Mimuluan, mind them to me."

But this technic Mimuluan knew of, was far more advanced. Answering Jadelain, she said …

"And that's the very thing there Jadelain, usually I would just simply mind them to whomever I wish to see, but with you, I have to make you see or visualise this method ..."

"Visualise this method?!... how will I do that?"

"Jadelain, the reason for this practice today, is simply only for one reason ...And that is to open your mind to what it already has deeply installed, your mind already knows of this technique...You Jadelain, are not fully awakened to it yet."

"I don't quite understand Mimuluan, I'm confused?? ..."

Mimuluan did not want to unsettle Jadelain again, nor make her fearful, so she simply stated ...

"Try to stay calm and focused Jadelain, I will clear the visual path for your mind to understand, but for now, we must hurry. I sense a disturbing fear of unwanted company, which is causing my mind to distract and lose focus of our task in hand...Hurry let's all of us lighten to my more secure, more peaceful settlement, you will find it easier, be calmer with the revealment within your mind."

Lightening to a more mutual ground within Trasuprimatul, the three continued with their attempt to manifest and evoke, the ability believed to be deep within Jadelain.

More questions were beginning to brew in Jadelain's mind, she was starting to become more intrigued with all the revealments.

She asked further of Mimuluan, "Mimuluan, Modyous spoke of my Indigenous people. There is very little to nothing I remember of them, but I have had over time, and more of recent, a slight curiosity or I am kind of intrigued to understand them."

This was particularly interesting to Mimuluan, perking up and answering Jadelain …"Jadelain… that is quite distinct. I say this as…"

Quickly though, Mimuluan knew she mustn't press.

"No, no… best we have less insight or interfering intuition from me. I am already having difficulty withholding my mind-ins as it is, which is already a confusion to me, very confusing indeed?" Jadelain answered Mimuluan, almost as though, she felt she knew what this technic was, what it has always been, no?

Stating to Mimuluan so obviously …"That is no surprise to me at all, Mimuluan?! We all know mind-ins can sometimes cause uncomfortable restraint on our minds, when trying to concentrate and especially when another is trying to sypher it."

Mimuluan looked straight to Jadelain. "See, Jadelain, that's the thing. No one is trying to sypher from me, not directly anyway and I am many a year experienced in this method, only few know of it, as its ancient origin, see only the best of all Dimensions' Seenhigh-Sypherers practise its complexed mental craft. My ability-discipline alone, has such mental agility, strength within my resistance to allow any to penetrate, but...."

"But what, Mimuluan??" Jadelain demanded.

"BUT Jadelain, whenever I am near you, I weaken immensely and what is even more confusing to me Jadelain..."

Mimuluan deadened her eyes with Jadelain, stating ..."Is the fact, that you are not even aware of it, and I have always asked myself, been plagued, intrigued with the prospect of...What if you were trying?!"

Modyous swiftly hushed the conversation, telling Mimuluan ... "Mimuluan, I fear, you have already said too much to young Jadelain. Please, if this-what you see, is not what you believe it to be, then already, we have jeopardised a greater outcome."

Suddenly Jadelain turned to Modyous, her entire person was entranced, a confidence, a power, rained from her, both Modyous and Mimuluan had never seen before.

Then Jadelain clearly said, "No Modyous, let her, let Mimuluan proceed with me."

Mimuluan knew instantly. "You already instinctively feel it, don't you, Jadelain?"

Mimuluan, feeling the ease within Jadelain, felt tremendous confidence instantly with what they were about to try, feeling that nothing could or would go wrong with her awakening of Jadelain's underlying ability.

She turned to Modyous, with a knowing confidence.

"See Modyous, you need fear no more, our inner knowing, 'my' second-sight intellect, was too strong, too permanent within both our minds."

She continued …

"Trust, Modyous, like you tell us all incessantly, all the time… like how you have just told Jadelain here today, and her (especially) because of the deep desperation and utter determination; you needed to convince her because you believe, strongly like me, she is far more relevant to the greater outcome for all, more than she even realised, and more so now, than ever before.

"Don't Modyous, let the doubt within your mind rule. For the first time Trasuprimordials must give in to mental intuition, driven by the faith of the heart."

Modyous succumbed to Mimuluan's reasoning.

"Yes Mimuluan, you are right, there is no need to question ourselves any longer. It is clear, we are starting to understand the way, that this is most definitely the right path we must pursue."

Suddenly Mimuluan felt Jadelain, her mind asked her.

"Jadelain, do you …"

Instant.

"Yes Mimuluan, I see you."

Jadelain had, could use this ability instantly.

With this explanation, both Modyous and Mimuluan felt a taming of calm and comforting ease, an unbounding from a relentless unremitting torment, this seeing them both near complete irresolute, within their finalising for their combined, much needed, agreeable, settlement.

Their relief stood.

Finally, they were both unmovable.

Then within that moment, Mimuluan, her body and mind easing, as though Jadelain gained the ability to comfort that part of her brain that irritably troubled her of Jadelain's possible ability to unwelcomely intrude her mind.

It was as if Jadelain could remove the doubt and fear about herself, in your mind, and manipulate your senses into trusting her invasion to your mental world, being only of a favourable, good-natured, better intentional, approach towards you.

You became convinced, she only had your best interests at heart, you believed ...more than her own.

Mimuluan felt compelled to answer whatever Jadelain's multiple questioning to her mind was, giving every answer with ease, no hesitation ...

... "Yes Jadelain, I see them too, I had pushed this memory of your kind so far, deep back into my thoughts, my mind wanted to protect me from...

... No Jadelain, these thoughts do not feel menacing for me...I will be more than willing to allow you to sight into them..."

Interference, sudden interference, Mimuluan could feel Jadelain had become overwhelmingly disturbed.

Panicking, she minded to her.

"... What is it Jadelain, what is it you ..."

Jadelain fearfully minded back.

"Vilier! Mimuluan... Vilier was your unease you felt earlier!"

Modyous immediately jumped up, asking, "Jadelain, you view them?"

"Yes Modyous, they will soon lighten here!"

Modyous ordered Mimuluan, "Mimuluan."

"Yes Modyous."

"Bring both yourself and Jadelain round to a mind-in that sees you both safe from any syphering. You have both deepened so much into each other's mental insights, I fear you are both too exposed and vulnerable."

Jadelain minded to Modyous, sorrowfully, "Modyous, I am so sorry, it is too..."

Suddenly, a film of sheer mind-in invasions coated the atmosphere, and a syphering of all three minds see them experience themselves concentrate a narrowing of combined mind control.

They all knew they had to collectively fight the imperilous intrusion, brutally, of their minds, to overcome the ultimate, overcome any mistakable release of mind-ins that could threaten them...

Threaten...

The Grid.

Then ...

The presence of a character, so wicked, shrewd and cruel, revealed itself.

"Modyous, Modyous, Modyous… there is no need to feel threatened. I am here with good will; I mean no harm."

Modyous recognised immediately, the mind that was assailing disruption, intrusively, to their three assembled and as the body of this mind materialised, delayed seconds after, Modyous answered discernibly, harsh, sharp tongued…

"Your kind know nothing of goodness… Kinlye."

The awful creature continued smugly, "Now, now Modyous, you do not even know why I am here."

"You did not ask for my permission for you to be here, that is enough to convince me, you mean devious, ill intent," Modyous spat.

Kinlye continued …"You know very well Modyous, you would have refused my request of any invite to see you and what I needed to inform you of. I could only relay directly to you."

Modyous was not about to give in to Kinlye so easily, he questioned him further, mindful not to fall for any skullduggery.

"So, what with your interrogating, forceful entry and your extended, bullyish pack."

Kinlye looked surprised, almost as though he really believed he was a genuine character and was truly shocked Modyous suspected him.

"Pack?" he questioned Modyous, almost offended.

"Yes Kinlye, pack. You do not deserve the term legion, which would give an impression far too honourable, that your kind are honest, sincere... even with each other...No, pack fits exactly right; like creatures of the dark, you only have use for who and what strengthens your individual success of complete destruction."

This statement, seemed not to move, nor bother Kinlye in the slightest. Shrugging, he continued ...

"Well then Modyous, I'd had better hurry in convincing you what I have to show."

Moving his hand slowly towards his head, whilst slightly sly-eyed, looking over to Modyous, making sure he had his full attention that this information he would convince, was of great use to Modyous.

Stating, "The mind-in I have, is of great use to seeing *your* kind remain firmly within The Grid."

Modyous puffed, not convinced, as he had been here before many-a-time with Kinlye. Letting Kinlye know this, he answered, "My kind *'especially',* why Kinlye, I feel honoured."

Modyous sarcastically replied ...continuing ..."I did not know, you held us in such high regard," he laughed.

Kinlye continued with his conceited display, this being with a confidence he never usually had, convinced he would win over Modyous.

He went on further.

"Modyous, we have always considered your Dimension as one we would highly regard for exception, by us, to save, should any near issue threaten you." This was answered by Kinlye, with such creepy, snake-like, grovelling undertones.

Modyous was not yet convinced. He demanded, "What is it Kinlye, you have to say? And hurry with it, I am already tiring with you."

Kinlye was feeling Modyous was subtly becoming intrigued, maybe he had him?

He continued …

"I cannot retail this mind-in, in the presence of all. The one that insighted me to this revealment, was surely confident, that when I spoke their name to you, you would need no convincing, even from one you despise, (so harshly I must add) like me."

Modyous condescendingly asked, *"And the name?"*

Questioning Kinlye… questionably?

Then minding-in, to the deepest depths of Modyous's mind, so fearfully careful not to reveal also, to all that surrounded.

Kinlye illuminated Modyous's mind with the visual of who it was that had sent him.

"You see Modyous," Kinlye followed…

"I didn't even mind his name, only a memory of his person I feel safe to show of him. If any here were to recognise him, then they also would be aware of what it is I am about to share with you."

Modyous wasn't impressed, he assured Kinlye assertively. "Kinlye, I will staunchly tell you now, as I do not want any confusion, or misleading by myself towards you.

"My intuition, my knowing of you, will never give me any confidence or belief in anything you say instantaneously. Make no mistake, I will always have doubt of you in my rational, balanced mind, let me stress this to you strongly.

"It is because, and ONLY because of your knowing, and I do not trust how you became such a being, that I will entertain your revealment," Modyous added.

"How you come to be the one to share this knowledge, whatever it is, with me, will always be my divine, from here on, determination, to find out how you came across it, and Kinlye if I find that you are scheming or attained this information through any kind of deceit, Kinlye, rest assured..." Modyous stated, "I will personally, relentlessly, drive and hound The Grid, for the wipe of you and your whole kind. Do you understand me?"

Kinlye smugly continued, minding to Modyous ..."Modyous, I am already confident you will trust this particular gained knowledge and can feel your favour towards me now, as I slowly reveal what I know of it. You too, can see Modyous, that it is of great interest to you and to all within The Grid."

Suddenly Modyous realised..."You have stopped the mind-in Kinlye, why?"

Kinlye looked over to Modyous, with a slight smirk.

"I have not stopped it Modyous, just stemmed it a little. I need to know; I have chosen wisely by sharing with your kind."

Modyous was not surprised, "No Kinlye, you need to know you will be repaid. What is your price?"

Hooked victory Kinlye had gained.

All was in his court, at his own leisure. He then proceeded to answer ...

"Modyous, wealth is nothing within The Grid, if you do not exist, and with times like...."

Modyous instantly shut down his glorified charade, blurting ...

"Get on with it Kinlye, WHAT is it you are asking?"

Kinlye continued, for he knew he had the upper hand.

"The confidence you have in our kind Modyous."

Modyous was confused, "What do you mean Kinlye?"

Kinlye went on ..."Well, Modyous, the same confidence you have of our kind, your opinion of us...

I am asking you have that same confidence, when approached by The Grid to vote...

'In' confidence of us instead."

Modyous was in sheer disbelief that Kinlye would even dare to ask this.

"You fiend Kinlye, and I do not believe you have not approached others with this...

Blackmail!"

Kinlye did not even bat-a-lid.

"Modyous, we choose to remain just like everyone else, just like yourselves."

He questioned … "Tell me Modyous, what was the reason 'She' is here?"

Modyous shut him down, instantly. "Kinlye, Jadelain is none of your concern."

Then Kinlye answered him, with a firm tone, stating the exact point he was trying to make.

"Of course, Modyous, we all just want to…remain."

As Modyous gave Kinlye a mind-in that assured him, there would be no revokes of his confidence vote to The Grid, should it ever arise for Vilier to remain. The other Trasuprimordial rulers of his Dimension, abruptly, in sheer panic, with their urgency to gain his attention, insisted he come quickly.

Modyous quickened the end of the encounter with Kinlye, but sternly warned him.

"Kinlye, I hope this is nothing of your deceptive doing."

Kinlye's confidence in his answer, was just too swift, to breathe, he hastily replied …

"I can assure you now Modyous, I am just as mystified as you."

Modyous was disturbingly unimpressed and replied with disgust …

"Even as your mind conjures the words, my body fills with doubt towards you, Kinlye.

You come with me. I am more than sure, whatever this is, it is most definitely linked to you."

Then suddenly. "Modyous!" sang (in unison) the other two rulers.

"Eathinua, Firaphin... What is the urgency?" Modyous demanded immediately.

Eathinua and Firaphin were clearly distressed, this becoming amplified by the presence of Kinlye!

"What is Kinlye doing here, Modyous? Why were we not informed of his coming? You know The Grid are becoming merciless with unannounced lightenings?!"

Modyous suddenly shot a sharp look at Kinlye, his eyes reading to him, the frustration and contempt for putting him in such a position, then he quickly turned to reassure the others.

"Firaphin, Eathinua, I can reassure you now, there is no need to panic, Kinlye had misinformation and decided for once, to do the right thing."

He said with slight scrutiny, whilst staring dead straight at Kinlye as he answered.

Modyous persisted in questioning the other rulers, "What is the threat, you all fear so terribly?"

The others continued, but their panic sore them talking over one another.

Modyous demanded, they speak one at a time ...

"You, Firaphin, tell me what the issue is?"

"Divinula, they are asking to lighten here."

Modyous' eyes flittered two, and threw, his mind, erratically thinking.

He commanded, "Then… let them."

Modyous then turned to Kinlye again. "From what I have seen so far Kinlye, I can assure you, the knowledge you have, I personally, will see it is syphered correctly in the favour for 'all' within The Grid. There is no need for you to be here any longer, but I will connect with you again."

Kinlye rapidly set to lighten away, answering Modyous, "Yes, I'm sure you will Modyous, careful though …Best not to link 'Her' in all of this."

Modyous ushered him and his crew to leave, his eyes scrutinising Kinlye with a look that intimidatingly stated, he was coming for him.

Kinlye looked him in the eyes also, with a breath pause, his eyes realising Modyous was not playing, then turning away.

Kinlye and his crew hastily made themselves scarce, exiting Trasuprimatul in a black ally, villainous, cowardly, manoeuvre, seeing they did not have to face and receive consequence for their 'yet again' disruption to another Dimension's upheaval and unwanted trouble.

"I know that is not the last we'll see of Kinlye, Modyous?"

Eathinua had grave concern.

"Eathinua, Kinlye is more in danger of 'my' newfound interest in him." Modyous attempted to reassure.

"Modyous, whatever it is, remember, Trasuprimordials think strategically, not with the heart."

"Oh Eathinua, there is a first time for everything," Modyous answered confidently.

"Oh Modyous, I am fully aware of *that*. Just make sure it is only used for that, that is needed of the heart," Eathinua shot back.

"When has my judgement Eathinua, ever been erroneous?" Modyous questioned, hoping for her confidence.

"Modyous, I instinctively trust you, should that instinct change within me…

Well, …"

Eathinua and Modyous' eyes met for an understandably, by both, breath moment, of the consequence 'if' ever a situation 'did' occur, where either were up for question…

Then Eathinua instantly brought back a peace between them, stating …

"But, for now though my friend…" Eathinua continued…

"Not yet."

Modyous speedily put aside the moment, commanding …

"Tell Firaphin to insight the lightening from Divinula. The sooner we clear their concerns, the better."

There 'still' was a greater concern for Eathinua.

"Modyous ..."

"Yes Eathinua,"

"Jadelain is still here."

Modyous felt no way of this, saying ..."I am fully aware of that, I will deal, best what comes to mind, the better approach to this ..."

Continuing, he said ..."Now please tell Firaphin to proceed."

Eathinua could do nothing but follow on with the command.

"As you mind Modyous, as you mind," she answered him.

Modyous headed to the secure placement made by the other rulers for Jadelain breathily before dealing with Divinula's imposing nosey visit.

"Jadelain??"

"Yes Modyous" ...

Jadelain's fearful concern was all over her person so obviously, as well as within, she was clearly unsettled and uneased.

Modyous speculated for a moment, what to do with her.

Then syphering his mind, puzzled, Jadelain stated, "I realise Modyous, you suddenly have changed your decision of my staying here."

Modyous desperately, in the short time they had, tried calming Jadelain's distress.

"I have Jadelain, to send you away now, will only cause suspicion by Divinula and a greater paranoia from The Grid."

Continuing on,

"No, no, Jadelain, you will remain. After all, your visit, this time, was purely without any designs of personal gain. You are simply visiting for your love of Trasuprimatul's unbiased judgement of all ..."

Asking her a rhetorical question, whilst still demanding an answer, "Are you not?"

Jadelain automatically read the madness within the method, stepping in line with it and answering immediately, "Yes Modyous, as I always do."

Now was not the time to question, she had no choice but to confidently have faith in Modyous' decision, though confidence, she most definitely did not have, she knew ...

This could not be shown.

As the nation of Trasuprimatul braced their selves for the arrival of Divinula, their four rulers, agreed, silently, mindfully, in unison, of their explanation, of Vilier's visit.

This needed to be, confidently, with no hidden doubt by any, delivered to Divinula, enough to convince them Vilier (for once) was here purely on good terms and…'she' also in good faith.

Divinula were not easy to convince but the credence they had of Trasuprimatul being of a moral Dimension, gave Trasuprimordials and their rulers the confidence, that they would be able to ease further unrest of this situation becoming unnecessarily chaotic.

Firaphin prompted Modyous of which Seenhigh-Sypher had been sent.

"Divinula have sent Ultenison."

Firaphin's concerns shot higher.

"This Modyous, is a situation that already to me, has a very volatile and great chance of a vicious outcome."

Modyous answered, with a sentence, neither easing, nor convincing, he would be triumphant in persuading Divinula they were not to be concerned, but his answer also stated truth.

His experience of Divinula knew they only needed slight excuses for interfering with others' affairs and that they genuinely were always just looking for reasons to use their (known by all) bully tactics.

Stating to Firaphin, "Firaphin, as Trasu are already practised in the mindset and motions or what triggers Divinula (Ultenison 'especially') we'll do what is necessary to avoid such problematic issues…that being what…instinctively and intuitively comes to mind …"

Modyous was making reference to their lust for destruction, but Firaphin was just too distressed to work this out.

"Why... you look so confused, Firaphin?!"

Modyous seemed to mock Firaphin's obvious delay in his mind of how they usually addressed Divinula.

Then reassuring him, Modyous volunteered himself to deal with Divinula.

"I..."

Modyous continued,

"will deal with them, the way 'I' always do...

Run with whatever eases or suits (at that given) their almost immediate simpleton settlement of convincing (on my part) explanation to their hot-headed, yet again, assumptions of others' affairs.

Once they realise, or their minds are convinced they have acted hastily again, it is not usually long after the incident, that all, will be swiftly put behind us ..."

Modyous went on ...

"The issue that concerns me most in all of this Firaphin... is the initial magnitude of the extended irritating riles that follow off the back of their rash, crashing intrusions.

"These are, most of the time, harder to gain reassurance within their minds, trying to get them to favour your explanation does require, slightly harder, manipulation, surprisingly enough, of their original concern (the more threatening, so obviously in the beginning).

One does wonder, that all Divinula need to act, is simply, a mind-in that confronts or questions their motives…

This, I am starting to realise Firaphin, is pretty much every counter-concern, from whoever within The Grid that does not see their visions."

He went on still …

"A relentless mission (on their part) to make an excuse of any encounter that does not agree (with them) giving Divinula reason to shut down and bully a submit, forcing the practice of their regime.

"And for some reason though Firaphin, Divinula choose not to want to control Trasu, instead, wish for us to forge a further allegiance with them, extended from The Grid, thus gaining complete control of 'all' within The Grid."

Modyous' sudden urge to blurt this statement made Firaphin a little queasy, as he felt now was 'not' the time for a lesson on Divinula.

Yet Modyous continued …

"So many times, I have been able to subtly persuade them away from this notion and although today is most definitely not for discussion of this, I will say Firaphin, it is becoming more arduous to convince them to not pursue their path of procuring complete oppressed control of 'all'."

Then almost as if to cut his rant, reader, Firaphin blurted …

"And yet... 'Modyous', with all, and I stress, all that you have relayed to me suddenly here in an instant, my comprehension of these matters, has great understanding, but my empathy in this given moment (I'm sorry to have to say) to acknowledge your slight unease to deal with this task, is slim to completely non-existent, and I'm sorry to sound so cold Modyous, but all that is worrying me so much right now, is whatever threat Divinula pose for Trasuprimordials, and I cannot urge you more to rapidly transform to whatever characteristics, Divinula feel better or are more comfortable with and trust you more in."

Firaphin answered unsympathetically cold, to the point.

Modyous, snapping back to reality, swiftly stated,

"I understand Firaphin. I have structured to all three of you, the mind-in I will relay to Ultenison. I will not create further more stress, changing any of all we have agreed, so suddenly, and all I ask of you 'all' is that you keep your heads as it is already becoming harder to gain focus of Ultenison and keep this what I am trying to mind to you all, separate; all-remain-in-unison-faithful-in-me-that-Ultenison-must-believe!"

The entrance that followed, so military-style exaggerated by none other than, their (Divinula's) most dramatic (all-be-it at times, entertaining Seenhigh-Sypherer) but by no means, could be underestimated and considered, extremely breakneck and high, hazardously, an extremely high risk...

Ultenison.

This was a character, a personality, that only a mad hierarchal organisation would give an immense level of power or authority to carry out critical and with high consequence danger, his poor decision-making rocketed his endless reputation for recklessly carrying out commands (some or most of them seeing him instructed to abought) almost, if not successfully, seeing sheer wipe or devastation to other Dimensions.

It was extremely hard for any to ignore or try to turn a blind eye to the most obvious flaws of this character, causing immense misfortune, widely throughout The Grid, the most common, his careless lack of concern for hungry, authoritarian, bullyish devastation, with no second thought for others.

This was clearly an eccentric, that had been given too much a free reign to live out his unrealistic reality, amongst real realists and their living reality of the cluster.

"Modyous!" Ultenison bellowed.

" 'I' came, (insisting that I be the one to, also to my board) ... straight to your assistance, those Villains only have one use and that is of a complete destructive agenda with no consideration for any other than themselves."

He continued to babble on ...

"I tell you Modyous, I do not know any other than that Dimension, that solely and wholly have nothing but devastation on their minds, you get my distress??!"

Modyous glanced, astonished, yet unsurprisingly shocked at the matter-of-fact statement loosely flung out there, with no hesitation (nor deliberate either) by Ultenison, and with slight sarcasm and condescending patronisation, he answered...

"Oh Ultenison, I am astonishingly puzzled, 'you' especially have not noticed my deepest concerns for, what is it you call 'them'??... Destructive, devastating Dimensions??" ...

Modyous continued with his condescending tone, "It does make me wonder Ultenison, if these particular Dimensions are aware of their own threat to all concerned?"

Ultenison's ignorance continued ...

"Modyous, I can assure you now, they are totally oblivion to their threat!"

"Oblivious... I think the word that you are looking for Ultenison, is oblivious, and you couldn't be more right. They are definitely, totally, clueless!...augh, and I can instantly see your cause for concern in this whole matter Ultenison."

Ultenison tried to answer Modyous with an authoritarian tone, but still sounding like a Bethune.

"You can see why, *'also'* Modyous, Divinula acted with such urgency and that with a military intel strategy in mind too!"

He continued to bore Modyous with his war explanation.

"War is always just right there on your doorstep, best to be ready for them at all times my friend, don't allow no sneaking up on you, catch you off guards, if you understand me?

"As you're aware only too well Modyous, you cannot take 'any' chances, especially now, as we all have to be so vigilant and in particular of those who are known to cause most suspicion ..."

And still ranting, he added, "And Modyous (and I really don't understand why you do entertain this character) the main concern in all this unnecessary affair, is 'Her' link with all this. It just caused our radar to skyrocket off the scale."

"Ultenison!" Modyous exclaimed, and instantly minding to the other rulers of Trasuprimatul, demanding (what was unbeknown to Ultenison) their previous, before Divinula lightened, agreed explanation as to why Villier had come...why... 'She' was there also, simultaneously.

Modyous, risk-takingly went on to mind-in to Ultenison, the link that was confusing him so disturbingly, of Mimuluan, Villier and... Jadelain.

Modyous could feel-sense the unease of Ultenison's unwillingness to accept his reasoning. Ultenison never doubted this kind, for reasons coming purely from admiration and respect of the honour held so highly and widely known from all who knew Trasuprimatul, he would relentlessly find fault in opposing parties, rather than settle blame in them.

Modyous was fully aware of this most crucial fact and was relying intensely on its previous captaincy to sway Divinula... Ultenison especially and 'his' favour, for them.

Holding firmly (Modyous) and having complete faith in the other rulers, without the choice of using the ability to mind-check-in with them, what was a collective lie, with all four of them.

See, whenever Modyous had manipulated in the past, the truth, with anyone, let alone Ultenison, there was some real truth, even half-truth within the deception.

This time, it was fully, without an ounce of truth within it, a complete, fabricated lie, and Modyous had (with slight reluctances on their part) involved and convinced the others to playout this mania act.

Then...

"Modyous, I see it as clearly, my sky, third eye, those little...

And 'She' ...Modyous, 'She' is a part of it too!"

Without any hesitation Ultenison, seemingly, with sheer persistence within his actions, attempted to make contact with The Grid.

"I'll inform The Grid right away."

Modyous knew, he must remain calm, to lose composure now, meant the revealment of the others, of their deception, of the real reason 'She' ... Jadelain was there.

Overwhelmingly, suddenly, Modyous felt a relief, almost a release from his frontal mind.

And so calmly, Mimuluan took over. What was so stressful (hard in fact) for Modyous to convince Ultenison to believe, Mimuluan with her ability minded into Ultenison, mimicking Modyous's voice within his head, Mimuluan uttered, soothingly, a soft, quiet chant…

"Ultenison, never before have I given you reason to doubt me and that is also so today, with this given situation, you still should, and can remain confident and have no cause for concern… no doubt.

"I am going to share with you Ultenison, the reason why your mind is not settling with my explanation.

"Mimuluan, my most trusted ally, as you already know here on Trasuprimatul, has discovered a much unique and special, beneficial use for Jadelain."

As Mimuluan used Modyous's mind to gently coax Ultenison to accept the false truth, 'it' blindly being minded out to him so persuasively and convincingly.

Modyous most obviously knowingly, knew this was the particular ability, the one previously she had just used with Jadelain, who, to his stunned disbelief, 'She' (Jadelain) almost instantly learned to master.

Modyous wondered how she (Mimulan) was relaying, what was a little of a truth to Ultenison, without fully revealing the whole truth, also being able to do this whilst keeping both Eathinua and Firaphin confidently locked in, whilst also not revealing to them, the real truth of Jadelain, and as it seemed she was gaining favour by Ultenison to not inform The Grid of foul play. She calmly faded out of Modyous's frontal mind, allowing him to proceed with Ultenison.

"You see Ultenison, 'She' Jadelain, is very dear to us, we do not see her as a threat."

Finally, Ultenison was onside.

"Modyous, I can only say you're a fool for trusting a kind like hers!"

Modyous continued to ease him, losing his confidence at this point, would be a crucial and costly mistake.

"But Ultenison, did your kind not once work alongside 'Her, her Dimension in the honouring of a species, with their Dimension being of much use to The Grid, joining allegiance with us all."

Modyous desperately continued …

"This kind were the reason others joined us, making our force, stronger, sterner."

Ultenison had been tamed, yet again.

"I hear you Modyous, and I understand your reasoning. I will not call for the wipe of Zardinelle and I will not raise concern of Villier being present here.

I only hope you know what you are doing Modyous, I would not like to see the wipe of Trasuprimatul based on your trust in undesirables."

Modyous assured him.

"Ultenison, I am truly flattered by your concern, but you need worry no further, our kind, I can confidently reassure you, are in no danger."

As Ultenison and his heavily strong force set to highlight back to Dimension Divinula, Modyous was settled in his mind, that once again, he had convinced peace-in-mind of Ultenison, rather than blind-brute-force of destruction.

The four rulers, immediately, set to relay, in unison, that peace had once again been restored, using their ability of minding into the nation of Trasuprimordials', their citizens, the ease within their minds, and collectively, calming and putting to rest, almost eliminating their fears and anxiety, fading out as if never existed, the memory within them all, of this disturbing incident.

"I only hope Modyous, that this event, is put swiftly and firmly behind us," Eathinua stated.

"Eathinua, I'm afraid, I cannot promise you that. Villier, whether intentional or not, have presented me with a task so arduous and demanding, so burdensome, with no choice for me, but to pursue and make certain the outcome from the little I did see of their knowledge is delivered, with favour for all our Dimensions," Modyous answered.

"Surely Modyous, it is not that exaggeratingly menacing?"

"If my instincts see my disturbed fear of this right, then Eathinua, the threat spans beyond The Grid, I feel the whole Minlactic Cluster will be affected, I… Jadelain,"

Modyous was taken aback by her sudden appearance.

"Modyous… I heard you voicing to Eathinua your concerns, do you really fear a danger so great?"

"Jadelain, I do not know how great the effect of this mind-in will be, what I 'do' feel though, is that, if I do not pursue, I may regret."

Fading out of this deep memory of Trasu, unaware of the timeless fixation she had had of it,

Jadelain lay.

Deep in this memory of Trasuprimatul, her mind remembered a part within that encounter, of something lost or that she had somehow misplaced in her subconscious.

She concentrated on what she then, in that moment, did not realise.

Divinula always relentlessly, from her experience, wanted the wipe of her kind.

With that encounter, they chose… not to see the wipe.

This was significantly different.

Suddenly Jadelain drifted deeper into her mind, almost unconscious…

"If you see me now Jadelain, you're walking the right path."

"Him!"

Recognising the stranger and a vague remembrance of... the path...

Then suddenly, within that instant...

She woke.

Gone. Again.

No further forward, with no remembrance of what her mind had just revealed, Jadelain sat up.

The only sensation, instinct that came to her, was that... she must carry on.

Three: 3 Chapters In

"Directus Dujustious Liveniticus surely you can see from the abundance of evident mind-sighted mind-ins, collected and encased together (exhaustively, I might add) and with absolute rigorous, precise, thorough attention, my collective, my personal selected, investigate team, intricately structured, what has been put before you today. Surely, surely, Liveniticus ..."

"That's enough Genvia, you will address the board appropriately."

So not to confuse you, reader, a breathing (I shall give you) in past 'Law & Order' affairs within the lands of Sierephiar, a somewhat added entry to aid with the understanding of our story.

And now back to our journey ...

"That's enough Genvia, you will address the board appropriately."

Directus Dujustious Opseenision ordered.

"Apologies Directus Dujustious Opseenision," Genvia promptly replied.

"May I continue?" she respectfully requested.

"Proceed."

Genvia continued ...

"Please understand, all who I stand before today, please, it is only because 'I' and I am strong in my belief, my confidence in these insights."

Her distress in her desperation to gain confidence, gain favour, was becoming more apparent.

She suddenly became flustered.

Directus Opseenision, could see this clearly. Easing her, he stated ..."When you are ready, Genvia."

Genvia, took a breath, gathering herself, calmly, she continued ...

"I see clear, know vividly, that the one who stands before you on trial today, will be, is, the only, the main cause, the destruction, which will not only bring down the land we stand in, but will most definitely be the wipe of all within The Grid and most certain those surrounding."

Genvia went on, her voice, stern and heard in her incessant insistence, that her Board 'must' with no other option, adhere to what she was proposing this day.

"They must be punished, and most definitely must not be given any more free reign, or chanced ability in bringing down The Minlactic Cluster."

She proceeded with a definite tone.

"They must be expelled to O, this being the lenient of punishments put before them."

Aware that the whole of Sierephiar were minded-in and knowledgeable of 'all' the evidence put before them.

The floorless obvious verification, corroborated, certified, with no way of swaying a doubt within its accurately placed presentation.

The Board of Sierephiar needed very little to no time, to decide, let alone discuss, whether The Grid should be informed and encouraged in joining them in the decision of punishment for the said accused.

All waited anxiously in the land of Sierephiar, a cold silence followed ...

"Globelious, stand," Opseenision ordered.

Globelious slowly, with an unmoveable care, though knowing of his situation, a careless, reckless arrogance, a confidence that struck a fear, for how could one still have a stance so certain, so sure, even with an inevitable fate, facing.

Directus Dujustious Opseenision proceeded with the order.

"You are here before The Board of Sierephiar.

The decision has been made collectively among us, agreed also by The Grid and the power to rule the sentence that has been put over you today."

The Board stood.

Opseenision continued ...

"Board Directus Dujustious; Liveniticus, Opseenision, Pollilitenous, Clearcrienesium and Quitetolian, sentence you to eternal excel to Dimension Obuseencentfinitus, where you will still serve our Grid, but as a Dimevice-Addictator."

He finalised, "This is official. This is stated."

Globelious stood stern, a steel within his stance, hard confidence, a convincing agenda which followed in 'his' statement to 'all' …

"Yes Opseenision, yes, I will go to O, gladly and honourably, with all, I can now, with no shame to hide, admit, that I, Globelious, can, and will see, the permanent destruction, of all within The Grid, and I hope, especially, agonisingly, for those who reside on this Sierephian Land."

The chill that exited with his unnerving, tyrannical exterior, sent a cold across Sierephiar.

No 'one-mind' uttered their relief, no 'minds-combined', would ever, forever, dare again.

As the Board prepared to clear and file the evidence used in the long trial before them, Opseenision was approached subtly by another Board member…

"I hope Opseenision, you have agreed for the right decision."

Opseenision turned quick to face the one who dared challenge The Board, The Grid.

Standing before him was the obvious, he'd already known.

Addressing the individual with no scrupulous sympathetic tone, instead, a disgruntled tone Opseenision said,

"And I hope Liveniticus …"

(Spat sharply!)

"I hope, The Grid 'does not' see your relentless, consistent, reluctance to see the end to your friend."

Opseenision viciously continued …

"Be happy his only punishment was O …Be happy, you also, were not sent there."

Then ending abruptly with what he had to say, he finalised with …

"I never want to speak of this again. Be sure you never either… *Directus Dujustious Liveniticus*," Opseenision answered in a condescending, sarcastic tone, dismissing Liveniticus from his presence, with a cold turn show of his back and a silent wave of his hand to usher him away, like an annoying adolescent, irritating in his ear.

Liveniticus evaded this time, by a thin thread, a visit, (permanently, may I add also) to the dreaded dregs, within the pits of Obuseencentfinitus.

Later, when all had started to seem it was settling, Genvia visited Opseenision in his safe-occupied dwelling.

Opseenision (unbeknownst to Genvia) had company already, a *guest*, not favoured by Genvia.

Both Opseenision and his company already knew of Genvia's presence.

Genvia was not expecting Opseenision to be in company, so felt no need to mind-in before seeing him.

She had dropped her guard.

The visitor knew this, seizing an opportunity to mind-in to Genvia, an undermining, sarcastic jibe, knowing that addressing her this way would just taunt Genvia, making her feel incompetent for letting her guard down, allowing such an opportunity ...

"I can sense your mind already Genvia, stop with your bared-down, staunch persona."

The taunting voice went on ...

"Obviously, you are frustrated, angered even, with the final outcome of today."

Genvia, reluctantly went on to answer the individual, though, she felt the dislike of such a one and disappointment, that this person was present.

"Oh Clearcrienesium, funny, I didn't sense you here, but then how would I, you never want to be seen as directly agreeing to any questionable, especially, if first a conspiracy decision, until proven their vital significance and use for you," Genvia answered, with pure venom in her mind.

She continued ...

"One who never reacts, unless known fully, she is playing safe, with no chance of a comeback against herself... why are you here anyway?

"The Grid agreed to the Board's final outcome for such, the character Globelious was, and certainly deserving of his fate, surely you do not need still, to sneak to your verifications for your final decisions??... or is there something else needing to be stated?"

Clearcrienesium swiftly put Genvia, firmly back in her place.

"You, Genvia, are not as knowledgeable, or let me state this another way importantly informed as you think."

Opseenision immediately stepped in.

"Clearcrienesium, enough...

Genvia, all that could be done today, was done."

Opseenision shot a sharp eye to Clearcrienesium, a silent warning within it, demanding she quieten instantly, then instantaneously turned back to Genvia with a solemn expression, eager for her to understand, he had hers and the land of all Sierephiar and Sierephian kind, their interest, deep in his heart.

"Yes," he continued...

"Yes, you are not informed of all decisions made formally, you are not officially a Council Board Appointee. But Genvia, 'you are' a precious asset to our kind, and of grave importance and reliance to our remaining people. The sentence given today was just and efficient for the issues arisen."

Genvia continued to argue ...

"Opseenision, you can't possibly believe ..."

Opseenision, though reluctantly, had no choice, shutting Genvia down.

"Please Genvia, please, let's put it to bed and firmly behind us, no more will be heard, no more will be deliberated over."

Genvia stormed to the door, but before leaving, she turned, sternly stating ...

"I will willingly, never, speak of this again Opseenision, the single wipe of this official should have been made today, a zero chance of him ever completing his revenge."

She angrily continued, but it was heard in her tone, certainty ..."Yes Opseenision, I can promise I will never speak of this, of him, ever again, with any of you, but what I cannot promise, is that I will not deliberate over and over, of this, within 'my' mind."

The utter disappointment with her Board, leaving abruptly, her stomach churned, twisting, she felt emotionally betrayed.

Unsettled, unsatisfied, unfinished.

Inside, Clearcrienesium, seized an opportunity to pick Opseenision's ear, his conscious ...

"You really 'must' remind her, her position, Opseenision."

Opseenision looked out, watching Genvia fade into the night. He turned, sighing, reminding Clearcrienesium ...

"Her position is why we have remained so long."

And now...

Outlaws, complete habitual breakers of 'Law & Order' ...

"What was the outcome?

Are we formally asserted within The Grid... Liquylor?"

Vilier came to be a nation on The Grid, through sheer deception, trading information with O's Dime Agent, Liquylor.

Liquylor was a creation made by O's Dimes, their personal form of Seenhigh, to deceive and retain vital, valuable, particulars-deeds of other, more weak Dimensions. Easier pickings for the Dimes to gratify their compulsion to feed their fixation on ultimate wipes.

Addicts was what Dimevice-Addictators amounted to. Sent from whatever Dimension or The Grid itself, they were once important officials, so hungry though to abolish species of all kinds... even their own.

The Grid found a use for them, they would do the final deed.

If none else could be decided but the decision of wipe, a whole wipe of an entire Nation, an entire Dimension, Dimes were the ones who would finalise this despicable task.

Vilier knew of this, knew their hunger with this.

The Dime they had their sights set on, still had an ally.

They would, successfully, be part of The Grid...

No matter the consequence ...

And now back to our two favourites of all the characters ...

Or maybe not.

"What was the outcome? Are we formally asserted within The Grid... Liquylor?"

Eagerness to the point of desperation all over, within Kinlye's voiced mind-in.

"So hungry, too, are you Kinlye, you will be officially stated within The Grid very soon."

Liquylor's tone was sarcastic, taunting.

"But we ..."

Kinlye temptingly squirmed.

Liquylor instantly shut him down, she knew all too well, Kinlye's trait of trying his tongue to gain favour, she had grown tired of humouring herself with the façade of it.

"Oh no, not this time Kinlye, that is certified, you and your kind have done more than proven your ruthless ends to stabilise your permanent position within The Grid."

She minded directly to that part of Kinlye's mind, that faintly had reasoning, that knew there would be no two and throwing accepted by his deviating side.

She continued ...

"No... what my superiors want to know Kinlye, is whether you will remain loyal and your word, forgive me when I say this, isn't as strong as the behaviour you have displayed before now.

WeknowyouwillneverreturntoObuseencentfinitus, so, one more request is required of you...

'Her'..."

Kinlye knowing this would not be easily attained, asked frustratingly,

"What could you possibly want with Her??" ...

"Vital, very useful information, we know Kinlye, you are capable of gaining."

Liquylor's demands were clear.

"And then?"

Kinlye also, was growing tired of the charades.

"Then all will see."

Liquylor answered this with a kind of finalisation in her voice.

"What was the fixation with 'Her'? Why was, 'She' so sought after?"

Kinlye deliberated within his mind.

'Still' he thought

The wait would be worthwhile ...

Somewhere else, simultaneously (though maybe not at the exact same moment in each other's time zone) another event triggered by 'situational intuition' a universal, not personal instinct ...

Jadelain and her 'Him' encounter ...

"Jadelain."

Him.

This encounter, she felt different, she panicked, she stared, struggling to make him out, he couldn't speak, she couldn't hear him. His body was disturbed, she could only make out panic, unease in his body's movements, something had changed, the course of instinct to move had altered.

"What??!" she thought.

Jadelain was coming round, she was remembering, just slightly.

"Remember."

She thought.

"Remember the unease and clear discomfort you read Jadelain, from his body, his aura."

Snapping into consciousness, again, she envisioned his person, she would act on the meaning of what she understood, his movements were suggesting …

Brief, I know, sorry, and now …

Back to our two favourite villains …

(Come on, there's always someone out there who prefers the villains).

Minding-in to their Seenhigh, Liquylor, who was standing at the time, in the presence of Kinlye.

Dime-Addictator 'Highest' spoke to her mind.

"Is he aware why we want her?"

There was a pause, then Liquylor minded back.

"No."

Suddenly a twist in fate …

"Well now Liquylor, I'd better see that you get this precious information, soon. I can already see the importance of it."

Liquylor quickly gained focus on Kinlye.

"Yes Liquylor, they made you floorless in every aspect, one thing, unfortunately for you, your, compassionate consciousness... here... the lack of it."

Kinlye smugly continued ...

"See, you don't have the desires, the emotional ability we all have, to have a purpose, all you were made to desire, was information, you do not know why, you have not been made to care. You simply take orders.

Kinlye adjusted his posture, straightening his jacket.

Then ...

'He' continued, but to an order, preferred much for *and* by him.

"This is why your interior fails to read or instinctively understand, every time, when you should sypher out 'others' when minding-in with your superiors."

"Kinlye you ..."

Liquylor had slipped, a cost, that could be extremely costly.

"Now Liquylor, you know all too well, our kind do not do mercy, please, spare the pleading, our initiation to The Grid is well overdue."

Kinlyes eyes read triumph all behind them, a half-smile in tow also.

Liquylor instantly shifted the unease of Kinlye's realisation of her superior's agenda, addressing them with cold, hard, glass-cool composure.

"Kinlye has already confirmed my sighting, he has honoured our request."

"So soon Liquylor, are you sure?"

Highest was both impressed, also unsure.

Liquylor quickly eased his doubts, a must, after all she had no choice, the consequence of other, reader, I cannot even mention here on paper.

Answering him confidently …

"Yes Highest, knowledge he has of Her already, confirms my visions."

She then turned slow and serene, direct towards Kinlye.

"Be careful Kinlye, don't slip, there is already ways I envision, the others within The Grid want to wipe you."

Kinlye's confidence was also still very highly driven.

Replying to her, soo matter of fact. "Be careful and wise Liquylor, how you remain, so you can be here still, to see the wipe of us. I think that's what you should be concentrating on for now."

Liquylor laughed a laugh, sure she will soon catch Kinlye out, followed by …

"Ah Kinlye, that's where you are a fool, do you think the body that stands before you now, is the same you first met?"

She followed her statement, with a revealment, Kinlye should've taken into consideration as something extremely significant, given the nature of it and possible power (of Liquylor) within it.

"I have been regenerated and enhanced, with improvements, fine-tuned with nearly all the attributes of 'all' the different species, within The Grid and beyond, with only one trait separating me from you all."

Kinlye, still did not seem moved by her revealment, but asked his next question all the same.

"And what trait might that be Liquylor?"

Liquylor now fixated on Kinlye, knew he wasn't taking in the seriousness of what she had to say to him, this in her eyes, an easier chance to catch him out, his arrogance alone, would fail him.

She continued anyway ...

"Your relentless compassion to exist, so passionately, with 'all' your kinds, I pathetically add, and that I, unfortunately and annoyingly (for me) notice and have to endure of all of you."

Liquylor stared coldly at Kinlye, noticing the discomfort in the statement, directly made.

There was a frustratingly, strained length of time, before Dime Superior Highest returned the definite decision, that Vilier were firmly assured members of The Grid.

"There Kinlye, you have your desired wish."

She announced what Kinlye wanted to hear, but be sure, in her eyes, his time was already up.

Kinlye, true to form, gave an answer obvious of Kinlye-arrogance-style.

Putting *his* counter question to Liquylor ...

"You see, you should've asked me Liquylor, what my personal compassion and drive is with all this."

Liquylor looked at him puzzled, asking him ..."Oh... and what is that Kinlye?"

Kinlye turned facing her, arms stretched out, walking backwards, with a smirk on his face.

"The same as yours."

Then turning, running to lighten back to Vilier with the other unlikeable tribe, he turned quickly saluting Liquylor before they all faded out.

"Soon Kinlye, soon," Liquylor promised herself.

All the events within The Grid, that were occurring, still, were not piecing together, with an ability, for those who were trying to prevent the destruction of their own Dimensions and a decision or move, with a clear, beneficial outcome, they could make, with little to none, of any comeback, that would also bring complications to their people.

The land of Sierephiar was no exception...

"What is it Aliave? What is bothering you?"

Aliave suddenly sensed his mind becoming distracted, uncontrollably, for him, of a past encounter he had experienced many minds ago.

He could not make sense, nor understand why this thought, he did not ever see as of any importance and had immediately (at the time) dismissed, almost forgotten, why now, his mind seemed it had a significance to show him almost as though this memory would be the main influence on how he would approach and decide his actions with this run against their unexpected guest.

"Locline, whoever she is, she is not in favour of Sierephiar."

The mind-in visions were becoming stronger for Aliave, invading his ability to concentrate, trying not to lose his composure.

Aliave fought the pressure within his mind, he needed to stay focused, he needed to deal with this, swiftly, calmly, without any disturbance to Sierephiar.

Instantly without any notice, his mind shot him to the flashback it was insisting he acknowledge, it was vague, blurred, he struggled to make it out, whilst trying so desperately to fixate on her...

"Aliave!!"

"Who was this??" his mind rapidly questioned.

'She' ... The voice he could hear in his head, was trying to tell him, his mind... "She is ..."

Aliave instantly panicked.

"She is here to wipe!" he thought.

This was a warning, he instantly thought his mind was trying to warn him, this encounter all that time ago, was a warning for now.

Alterium.

Alterium was the place he met her, he still could not clearly make out the mind-in, but he vaguely made out her desperation, her anxiousness for him to see the danger of 'She'.

Jadelain also saw this vision, only, what she understood of it, was for the wipe of... Alterium.

Now understand, reader...

Aliave sees Genvia, Uliminous... 'Her' ... 'Her kind' ...

Genvia is distressed.

"What is it, Genvia?"

He tries to connect to the vision...

She must go! She must go!

And Jadelain is convinced, the calming voice she heard, just moments before her encounter with Aliave, must have been Modyous or Mimuluan.

Tackling it out with stand-off mind-ins with Aliave, Jadelain knows Sierephiar must go...

And well reader, we all know how that ended... need we really, to repeat that scene?

As she set to lighten home, she glanced up suddenly, him! unexpectedly...

"These events, you feel unsure of today Jadelain, may well be the unintended needed."

What did he mean?

How was this for the great of good??...

Something else came to light with this rencounter.

Jadelain realised, she was starting to remember her contacts with him... finally.

Four: 4 Chapters In

Deceivers, cold, no honour, no care, you slip, permanently gone...

Were you?

That being their code, understood, played out and delivered, just...

Among their own ...

Vilier and the Vilanian kind.

Much devious plotting reader, done between this lot.

The undoing of others, of each other, seemed to be their only goal, their sole purpose, and today was no exception...

"I'm not sold Kinlye, tell me, how will you convince *Queen Liquylor??!*"

This was said with pure sneering, mocking tones, followed by childish, simpleton sniggering from the other aloof members, sitting seemingly not caring for the conversation taking place, but be sure were (or thought they were) disguising their interest, should a piece of information slip, favouring them with the ability to gain 'upper hand-sudden power'.

This discovery (of that 'one day?' winning piece of information) between them, would be realised at most times, in unison and immediately, they would all be syphering one another (bluffing in short) out of each other's final attempt to nail success for whatever disorderly misconduct, they were dabbling in at that given moment.

Saying all this, they had all, also, grown, poker faces, distorting their features, making it nigh impossible for them to recognise each other, and especially …

their own selves.

Their pointless, infantile-style, heated congregation, continued with wasted energy, fuelled by interest only because, none had much else better to do at that moment.

The question, put before Kinlye tauntingly before of *'Queen Liquylor's'* convincing, was none other than Vilier's despicable leader …

Kinlye straightened himself, that way reader, we learned of him before, when 'he' is confidently convinced, he will win whoever he is addressing, over to his agenda …

stating'

"Well, Hyntightton, I'm glad you have the spare time to sit there, insulting me with your band of ridiculing buffoons, you must already have your plan B for when Vilier will finally face their ordeal of complete wipe?... Must be keeping it from us all, that's why he is so smug!"

Kinlye swiftly turned to Hyntightton's crowd of jesters, who instantly went from smirking goaders, to faces questioningly scrutinising their leader, with the thought niggling their minds... could he be planning to leave them all behind?? With a plan B.

Hyntightton slumped back in his chair, with a lengthened arm gesture and a wave of his hand.

"Go on then Kinlye, tell us your plan," he said in a breathless, effortless reply.

Kinlye leant in.

"Said one has still been leasing with the Dimension that sealed his fate, this I believe has been occurring also in complete unawareness of the rest of O's Dimes, this is an offence, even by their standards."

"And just how Kinlye, will this be of use for us?" Hyntightton's, impatient-irritatingly puzzled mind demanded, for even he was fast becoming bored of his lack of intuition for speedily understanding Kinlyes point.

"What is it Hyntightton, that Liquylor has always desired?"

Kinlye looked around the room, but all he was met with, was blank, mindless, clueless stares?

Rolling his eyes, he continued,

"Freedom," he blurted.

"She has always wanted freedom!"

"Go on Kinlye, I'm listening" Hyntightton gestured to him.

Kinlye continued.

"If we can relay this to Liquylor, giving her access to these precious particulars, thus giving her chance for her long-awaited release, we could persuade her to include us in the discovery of this said information, keeping us permanently secure in the eyes of The Grid, as a Dimension never to be suggested ever again, from any other Dimension, for any form of wipe, temporarily and most definitely, permanently, seeing The Grid also agree to Liquylor's permanent freedom."

"Well, well Kinlye, there seems no end to your cunningness, tell me though, how will you convince Liquylor to accept your lightening to O? When you were last there, you didn't exactly leave her with a confident impression you had her interests at heart."

Kinlye huffed, with his hand half clenched in a fist to his mouth and chin, and his mouth, slightly ajar in a smug smile, as he answered...

"I'll tell her, I have information of... 'Her'."

The group gathered in a huddle together and throughout the night and several nights after that, they skimmed and concocted their ruthless plan to manipulate Liquylor and finally see concreted, indefinite, stay, within The Grid.

Finally, Kinlye was ready to contact O.

Minding in to his much-needed contact ...

"Ah... You finally have something of use, funny, one comes along ..."

"What? ... Liquylor are you...?"

Liquylor cut through the response being answered-questioningly, towards her.

"Oh, nothing *Kinlye,*"

She answered egotistically conceited, supercilious even.

"I cannot wait for your return, and finally 'all' have very useful booty, 'especially' for me".

Kinlye was puzzled by Liquylor's response.

"All," he thought.

But he did not ponder on this for long, he had his required answer.

He would immediately set to lighten to O, time was most definitely not on his side.

Vilier and their leader were keen to see him off to 'O'...

"Kinlye, are you ready for us to mind-in to Liquylor, for your lightening?"

Hyntightton eagerly asked.

"Yes Hyntightton, I am more than ready," Kinlye answered.

"This was the plan," Kinlye thought.

That would finally deliver (for Vilier) their ultimate intention, successfully.

"Do not fail us Kinlye," Hyntightton ordered.

Following with his orders to Spineleath, Hyntightton continued ...

"Spineleath, guide him steadily to our victory."

Spineleath assured Kinlye, all was good to go, stating ..."Liquylor has responded Kinlye, all you need do now brother, is jump."

"Done with pure perfection Spineleath," Kinlye complemented in his reply.

He continued … "You linked with her seamlessly, do you think she was able to mind from you, our plan?"

Spineleath confidently and conceitedly answered, "She was completely oblivious."

Kinlye set for his jump, so far, so good.

But as he transported through to the last part in his advance towards Obuseencentfinitus, he realised quickly, that there was a distortion with his mind-in, he was channelling to Liquylor.

He instantly tried to mind back to Spineleath, but he was already disconnected from him, from Vilier.

His mind deliberated, had he been duped, was this a double crossing?

With no way to double back, his mind flickered rapidly, trying to materialise a warrant, an agenda for his jump, that he would have to plead with Liquylor, with O, seeing that he would be able to leave and return to Vilier unscathed.

He would deal with Hyntightton just right, when he returned.

Right now, though … stay alive.

Back in Vilier, Spineleath was in pure turmoil, for he had also realised, something had gone terribly wrong.

Only he thought?...

'He' was the one who had lost the connection.

Sheer panic.

He had to compose himself swiftly, the others could not read this from him.

"Has our friend landed safely?" Hyntightton demanded from Spineleath.

"All went well from this end," Spineleath speedily replied.

Hyntightton's expression showed he was satisfied with his answer.

"Good," Spineleath thought.

They did not detect.

Deep, cavernous in his mind…"Hurry Kinlye."

Kinlye felt an unusual confusion, a strange sensation, he knew-was sure, he was in grave danger in O, but something was wrong and not a wrong where he felt threatened either, no, instead, he felt hidden, almost as though he had a cloak upon him, then Kinlye realised…

He had lightened undetected.

Quickly registering what had happened here, Kinlye laughed to himself.

"Spineleath, you old fool!" he thought.

Kinlye intuitively knew what had happened, see, his kind were used to attempting jumps and attempting them, when other Dimensions' Seenhighs were also making a jump.

Vilier were always exercising this act and so sneaky they were with it too.

"Just think," Kinlye thought to himself smugly. "And we've managed to execute this jump too, so well also, and we didn't even mean to!"

But now Kinlye was mystified to see who else was at O and feeling much more brazen than ever before (and especially knowing he was undetected) his devious mind was just too curious and his uncontrollable urge to know, took over and he set to see (or more to the point) if he could possibly gain from this other encounter.

Kinlye trekked further forwards, following his instinct for direction, whilst also making sure he did not become detectable, suddenly, a mind-in, but how? Who?... Kinlye instantly locked into the encounter of the two, a greet already deep in its conversation. Listening in, he attempted to make sense of what would seem was already in full flow of an informative, agreed and finally, finalised outcome of and for the two parties ...

"And you're sure 'She' is the connection?" the first asked.

"Oh yes," the other reassured.

"You have exceeded yourselves today, I will see you are rewarded greatly for this fruitful exquisite piece of intelligence."

"Ah, Liquylor," Kinlye thought deeply.

"And you," ... he thought also of the other party.

But Kinlye knew there was little time. With his experience of these kinds of jumps, he only had moments before they both would detect him.

He immediately set to find a safe place to channel back to Vilier, Hyntightton would be more than happy with his new find.

This would most definitely see them clear of any chance of wipe and potentially see them stand tall overall and possibly see them ruling 'all' within The Grid.

"Spineleath."

Kinlye minded-in to him, careful that his contact was not perceived nor imperceptible.

A lengthy pause, then suddenly...

"Kinlye, thank god, please tell me you are ready to lighten home."

Spineleath demandingly asked,

"Oh yes, my brother, and with a bounty, not even Hyntightton himself could find floors to ridicule, now bring me home friend, with a certitude, so swift and confident, we will never have to make these expeditions ever again."

Once back at Vilier, Kinlye knew he was home dry.

Time to make Vilier once and for all, top of 'all' (within The Grid) Dimensions.

When Kinlye finally relayed back to his Major General and Officials, his significant, valuable, findings, it was rapidly realised, this incidental discovery, would prove extremely useful, in very near time also, and was indispensable-priceless even, and very fast amongst the group, a bold bought of reckless, arrogance, moved dreadfully throughout, and their heartless leader stood with a cold confidence, stating…

"We will immediately set out all and every one of us, to every and last Dimension and they will, with certainty, give their last breath for this find, but we will be smart, we will gain first, their assurance, that we will no longer be an option for their individual choices for wipe, we will also have them agree, that because it was us 'personally' who gained this from said one …"

Hyntightton was abruptly interrupted by Kinlye.

"But I did not hear this explicitly stated by 'said one'," Kinlye blurted.

Hyntightton continued with a confidence, completely ignoring Kinlye's concern and sure once he heard this next part, Kinlye would no longer be concerned either.

"No need to worry little brother, once all within The Grid and The Grid itself hear that one of ours had learned and decided to share with all, no one else will ever question our honour and as for O and their ever-violating Dime, The Grid and all within it, will most definitely, no doubt, see the wipe with him and his artificial little Seenhigh… Liquylor!"

All knew simultaneously what needed to be done.

Start of the deviating, persuasion of the other Dimensions, it was time to gain favour.

First…

Trasuprimatul.

Five: 5 Chapters In

"Modyous is definitely a tough cooky to budge."

"But do you think he will fold to our will, Kinlye? That is the question."

"Once all the other Dimensions succumb to our proposal Hyntightton, Trasu will soon follow lead. Don't worry Modyous is just a minor irritation at the moment. Make plans, speedily for our next visit."

"Where do you intend to strike next, old friend?"

"Divinula seem a good catch for our second haunt, don't you think?"

"Clever Kinlye, a very strategic move. With the two, once firmly on our side, The Grid will soon be siding allegiance with our kind."

"Then Hyntightton…Complete Control!"

Fresh…

For such a recent unite to the ranks within The Grid, Divinula had certainly stamped their mark and done so *also*, with assurance to other Dimensions, that theirs was of a stern intolerance of any who did not follow (like their own) the stricken rules of 'non-threatening commitments' towards one another or The Grid.

This they displayed clear and made understood, with decisions, frequently made and final with that, for entire wipes of other Dimensions.

The Grid (fortunately for others) were heedful and vigilantly aware of this unscrupulous trait, and see in early experiences of these, that any suggestions made by this Dimension 'particularly' were thoroughly scrutinised before any conclusions were decided off the back of their say.

Divinula, in such a short space of time had acquired a vast amount of cognisance, learned with a mastery so excellent in their delivery, from other and more ancient Dimensions.

Mind-in techniques was their obsession, and perfection with these was their ultimate determination, but at what cost??

You see, they did not and had absolutely no intentions of adapting the philosophies of these ancient counterparts, which were that you only used these, enough to see your Dimension free of any possible threat and you 'only' used the power (against others) of these, when nothing else was an option, should 'any other' pose a threat to you or your kind.

They were going to master these, using them with the sole intention, to conquer (though stated by themselves, not for their own sole gain) a 'one united order for all' within The Grid.

This ideal was also shared by... Rotherillia.

And here on this fine day in Divinula, reader ...

"Hyntightton is requesting a jump here, Ardillion?"

"Hyntightton?! He's a brazen beast, asking to even be considered for a possible invite here.

Finally lost his twisted mind! Ha ha."

"Should we refuse him?"

"Oh no Blenim, you accept that request good and now, for Hyntightton to have the bold, courageous mind to even think of asking to come here, tells me he believes he has something so good, that not even we would refuse his proposal.

"No, you tell him, we're more than happy to see him, he may have useful information and I don't want to be regretting that I didn't take up a chance to learn it and if it's something coming from Hyntightton...It's likely to be something that can be used against 'us' at some point."

Back in the savage fest of Vilier...

"Divinula have accepted Kinlye."

"Well, well... Ardillion must be deliberating long and hard for what we have to reveal, probably threatening deeply for whatever our intentions."

Kinlye spat this with a ridiculing, taunting tone.

Hyntightton met it with a jester-like, mocking reply...

"We should make him wait, stew a little!"

They both sat in their newfound glorified accomplishment of attaining or soon to be attained, upper hand of not only the lower levelled of the

Dimensions within The Grid, but possibly over the more influential Dimensions also, and both knew silently between the two, this newfound power, Vilier were not going to use slightly or with any remorse.

The revelling, shared by both, for sheer contempt and definite torment for every other Dimension, they enjoyed in that moment, savouring every painful (that they were going to inflict) thought of what they intended to do.

Now back to war hungry Divinula...

"Have you lost your mind, Ardillion?!"

"It would seem so Marshillarn, but you just take a moment here to think about why I accepted this jump."

Ardillion slumped back in his chair, arms folding over comfortably, slowly-confident.

"Explain Ardillion, half the board and frankly the whole of Divinula were wondering why such an outrageous request has been approved and so breezily by 'you especially'??!"

Marshillarn was unimpressed.

Ardillion questioned, a rhetorical question.

"Do you not think it strange that *Hyntightton* would request a jump here and by 'me especially' as you so put it, and also (which is widely known) my disapproving of such a character?

"Think Marshillarn and think hard. What could it be that Vilier have and feel so confident, that not even 'I' would refuse them for it?"

Marshillarn paused for a breath moment, then looked back at Ardillion with an expression that showed the same realisation.

"I will immediately set for Ultenison to meet with them," Marshillarn was swiftly on board.

"Don't want to send Blenim to greet them then, Marshillarn?" Ardillion teased.

"No way, the sharp ruthless, intolerance of Ultenison is what they'll be given, and he will not be by anyways greeting them, a meet is definitely what this will be and a swift, raw deciphering one too. Whatever devilment they're up to this time, we'll duly get to the bottom of it quickly."

"Now you're talking my language Marshillarn, prepare Ultenison right away, this could possibly be the excuse we need to wipe that kind once and for all."

Once Vilier had received their confidant confirmation to go ahead with their mission towards Divinula, they meticulously set out their strategy, syphering to their lead Seenhigh, Kinlye, the precise order of how he would mind-in the specifics of the particular information they had obtained, using (when they finally would deliver this information) manipulative and very persuasive methods, done so many times before. Only this time, the crucial importance of this intelligence, they knew, could not be rejected.

"The right Seenhigh has been selected, as we predicted, to greet me."

"Yes Kinlye, just as you foresee...Ultenison."

"His obvious simpleton mindset is just the right amount of stupid we need."

"You're sure he will buy it?"

"I know he will, anything fed to him, to his hungry mind's obsession to remain on The Grid permanently, completely blind sights him and distracts him from ever questioning others. I can tell you now, with ultimate confidence, he will not even mind-in for a second opinion."

"Careful, as you sypher though Kinlye, Divinula have many an undertone of strategies, when it comes to others and 'us' especially."

"Yet Hyntightton, they send Ultenison and further still, accept our proposal. I am not fearful at all for a threat of Divinula and I do not feel that any skilful form of syphering is explicitly needed on this visit. This will be very short and very sweet for our gain."

The atmosphere and the energy Vilier could feel, once consciously entering Divinula, menaced and jived at their exterior.

Composure was at its highest, in trying to 'not' show, second-thought processes of any kind.

"Hold your guts, the lot of you, you're weaker than rolling steel under mind pressured controlled heat.

I tell you now, I will sypher you all to a mind-in heap, you will not ruin this, *so far* into succession,"

Hyntightton spat.

Divinula prepared for the lightening of Vilier...

"To the Arkle Lake as you intended, Marshillarn?"

"No."

Marshillarn doubled back on his decision.

Peakia looked confused.

"Then where??" she asked.

"The Bountine Drop."

"But you told them" ...

"Hush Peakia, Ultenison is waiting to greet them, and also...

Blenim."

Kinlye minded-in to Peakia.

"Highlight us to Arkle Lake, Peakia."

"Ah... no Kinlye, Bountine Drop is where you will be highlighted."

Panic instantly overcame Viliers crew.

"Keep your heads you fools or I'll ..."

Kinlye spun back to his mind-in to Peakia.

"Careful Peakia, this move could more than cost you the vitals I have, any sense of double crossing ..."

"No, no Kinlye, it was thought best, the meet be there."

"And every thought process from here on Peakia, I advise be done with due caution," Kinlye advised, demandingly sharp.

Peakia part closed her mind out of her connection with Kinlye, minding-in with...

"Ultenison, we'll all three, you, me and Blenim, need to sypher-out Kinlye in unison. Ardillion insisted he must be lightened here before the reveal of Blenim."

"Then highlight him fast Peakia, let's not disappoint," Ultenison ordered her.

Peakia instantly set the highlight.

Tension was high, the two finally met.

"Kinlye."

"Ultenison."

"Reveal yourself brother, I only feel your voice."

Kinlye revealed in physical, solid matter from the shadows of mind-in visuals.

"Ah, there you are Kinlye, such a long time my friend."

"Blenim! what is ..."

"Calm Kinlye, Blenim is only here to assist, just as you have yours."

"Ultenison, let me just show you a glimpse of the nature of why I am here, maybe then all this foolery will stop."

As the meet between Kinlye, Ultenison and Blenim took place, simultaneously across land, Ardillion, mind-linked between Peakia, who was part mind-linked to Ultenison and Blenim, them, having to painstakingly keep Kinlye out of the mind-loop, that Ardillion was also linked to Divinula's close allies...

Rotherillia.

"Now Kinlye you tell me right away, how you came across such crucial particulars?"

"More to the point Ultenison, should you not be asking me, how such familiars would be of use to yourselves?"

"You did not reveal all you know, Kinlye."

Interruption...

"Ah... Ultenison!"

"Not now, Blenim..."

"The rest, Kinlye,"

"But Ultenison,"

"Shut up and be quiet Blenim! Kinlye, I'm giving you" ....

"Come now Ultenison, I can feel your mind buckling from the multiple mind-in links, far and wide, and Blenim isn't making it any easier for you."

"Why won't you show me the rest?"

"I need assurance, Ultenison."

"What kind?"

More interruption.

"Ultenison you really must listen ..."

"Blenim!" Ultenison spat.

Mind-syphering Blenim and the numerous links, also minded-in to the meet, Ultenison completely blocked all connection from himself and Kinlye.

"Name your price, Kinlye."

"I knew I could count on you 'especially' Ultenison."

"Speak your ask, Kinlye."

Ultenison was becoming fast impatient, frustrated and annoyed.

"Complete exclusion, from your kind of our kind, ever being suggested for wipe ever again, and I can assure you my brother, your kind along with whoever else joins us in revealing this to The Grid, will be guaranteed ultimate immunity also."

"Ultenison no!" Blenim spat.

"Done."

Too late, Ultenison had already agreed.

"Thank you, my friend, your concealment binds more than ever before."

"Ultenison," Blenim uttered his name this last time, with breathless defeat.

"What is it Blenim?"

"Ardillion warned Kinlye would do this."

"Why didn't you tell me before, you idiot?!"

Blenim shook his head, "Ultenison, I do not know what you have agreed to, I can only hope friend, it is not too damaging and Ardillion can break its bind."

Ultenison gave Blenim a look, neither concerned nor reassuring, a dead stare was all that could be read, for Ultenison, true to form, was only driven by pure might and any chance of limitless control and ultimate rule throughout The Grid.

Unfortunately, though, *seen* with this... was the problem or concern that 'all' within Divinula had, and 'that was' … at what cost to Divinula 'also' and most important of all, at what cost to…

The Grid.

"Ardillion, your man, *Ultenison*, is becoming quite a nuisance and a known spectacle."

Ardillion attempted to talk his way around the statement…

"Quatesok, I can reassure you now, he …" Quatesok cut him to the quick.

"Save it Ardillion, it's embarrassing, rein him in and fix this… immediately."

Rotherillia's leader, a spine-splitting ruler and chilling, unnerving dictator. He was not by any means, known for patience, of any kind, nor mis-happenings or thoughtless mistakes, from his own, his, and especially any associated with him.

Quatesok, instantly cut 'any' kind, individually or collectively, from his favour, from just slight disappointment. No scruples this character had and most certainly no sympathy for any who did not meet his criteria of absolute, seamless, superiority of convicting any given order by himself or linked to himself.

Perfection was the agenda and perfection was all that was expected.

"Damn that Ultenison, Minkai!"

Minkai, was the only saving grace for Divinula in 'this' given situation and the 'only' saviour within The

Whole Grid, when any were dealing with Rotherillia and Quatesok.

A second to Rotherillia's Dictator and a confidant and 'only' voice able to liaise or converse with Quatesok.

Minkai (fortunately for others) had a softer interior to one's ruler, the yang aura that embodied her, was so purified, that Quatesok would uniquely consider any order he made, and if convinced of, (maybe) ever changing it, 'it would' and only 'should' come from her.

Quatesok, tired of yet another failure from Ultenison, sending Minkai to deal with Ardillion,

"You know Ardillion, the only reason he is even considering your allegiance right now, is your shared views. You are on very thin ice with his interest to be associated with you, but then again...his adherence to any, is thin-iced, questionable, universally, don't you think?"

The two shared a quiet chuckle for a slight moment before moving swiftly to more serious, pressing issues, that both Rotherillia and Divinula shared deeply, collectively, of 'others' within The Grid.

"The Grid 'must' be convinced, and soon, of our concerns Minkai and what 'I' in particular caught of 'Her'," Ardillion pressed.

"Yes Ardillion! I caught wind of that too, in Ultenison's mind-in with Kinlye?!"

Minkai added.

Ardillion laughed a condescending tone, almost patronising of...

"Ultenison, he's such a fool! Ha ha."

Ardillion continued...

"You can always count on him to botch things up, this time though, he's actually been useful!"

"This isn't an issue we should be laughing about though Ardillion, seriously now friend, what do you suggest we do?"

Minkai was serious.

"Track Kinlye," Ardillion said at once.

"I agree," Minkai followed.

"Wherever he goes Minkai, we must make sure he does not make it to Zardinelle or...

'Her'."

Six: 6 Chapters In

"I have spoken to Minkai, she has informed me of the order you intend, how will we be convincing The Grid *we* should be the ones to orbit to 'O'?"

"Firstly… 'I' will be the one convincing of my intent to send you to Obuseencentfinitus, you my dear Risauma, make sure you relay mind for mind my exact dialogue I want for my chosen Dimevice-Addictator, no room at this point for 'any' misread nor misunderstood instructions… I will have zero sympathy for any one bodied failure, is that clear?"

"Yes, Quatesok."

Quatesok dismissed Risauma from his presence, with an eye contact, known only by his agents, a silent command, but very direct in its delivery.

Quatesok knew his proposal had to be convincing and enough so that The Grid would also see his Seenhigh-Sypherer orbit to such a place as Obuseencentfinitus.

"What do you intend to tell them?"

Minkai waited anxiously, as Quatesok deliberated on his answer.

"We will tell them exactly what your mind sees."

"But how will you convince them *our* Seenhigh should go?"

Quatesok stared at Minkai, almost as though he was looking into the part of her he trusted the most. It seemed that for the first time, his long glance was searching, begging that connection with her, asking desperately, that she please, not let him down, that this time, more than ever before, he needed her honesty, her loyalty, he needed to know, he could trust and trust with no ounce of any doubt he would usually conjure deep within his mind.

For the first time, he was putting his better judgment into the hands of another, vulnerably and chance-takingly, riskily.

"I know said one Minkai, and I know him well."

Quatesok was serious.

"I know," she replied.

"No Minkai... I know him personally."

More serious Quatesok was, in what he was stating than his usual stance.

Then minding into Minkai, an encounter, pushed deep down in the depths of Quatesok's mind, he revealed a hidden memory that he had kept, shielding all these years, from everyone... even from Minkai.

As this memory entered her mind, flooding her sensations of her acknowledgement and the awareness of it, fear swarmed her body, and she knew instantly...

"It will not be Risauma Quatesok, that will be addressing The Grid...it will be me."

Minkai understood the seriousness of this revealment instantly.

"So, you understand my concern," Quatesok desperately asked.

Minkai's mind answered directly to Quatesok's.

"This must be executed Quatesok, with the urgency, exactly as your mind revealed to me."

She continued…

"The Grid will 'insist' it is only us that should orbit to O, and they will insist…

We most definitely 'should' orbit to O."

"Make plans Minkai my child, you are going to The Board of The Grid."

The orbit to The Grid was intense and concentrated for Minkai especially with this visit.

Her focus was one so much more fixated and cautious, in a narrowed-visioned, her sight, kind of way.

She felt instantly, upon arrival, the questioning-doubt amongst the citizens of officials within The Grid, but she knew, she must not waver, must not show an indifference of what she came to ask, nor reveal what recent knowledge she had just gained.

Her confidence was stronger than ever, she would be leaving today, with favour from The Grid, that her kind, would be orbiting to O.

"Well now Minkai, this is a revealment from Quatesok, shocking even for one like me."

"So, you see Directus Dujustious Minelord Byston, we must orbit, and urgently."

"Instant passage will be given, immediately, from The Board of The Grid, I hope your Seenhigh-Sypherer finds their Dime in good time and good form."

"They will execute this visit with all the certainty and urgency we all have for this mission to successfully, follow, triumphantly."

With that, Minkai immediately made exit to her Dimension.

There was no time to lose.

An orbit to Obuseencentfinitus, was swiftly needing to be ordered and accomplished, Quatesok now had his go ahead, he required.

Once back in Rotherillia, Minkai headed straight to Quatesok's Dictocan General Headquarters.

"Do you feel Risauma is the best choice for this crucial visit to Obuseencentfinitus?"

"I know, the significance of this, is fundamentally damning should even the slightest detail go wrong."

"Can I remind you Minkai, to 'never' oppose my decisions in my affairs and as for you Risauma… you are not giving me confidence in your ability to execute this triumphantly, and unfortunately, in that, I have to agree with you both, I, we, have got to, strategically and painstakingly, fine comb, mentally through this."

Minkai and Risauma, in unison, glanced in both shock and unexpectant surprise, as not only did Quatesok not answer with a usual intent to strike fear into his drudge labourers, one of Minkai questioning Quatesok's decision to send Risauma and two,

Risauma also questioning the decision and also one's ability (chosen by Quatesok) that one could deliver, even with self-doubt, but it seemed he was maybe suggesting they aid him in his decision in what way to approach O?

This made both an excitement and also uneasy reaction leave their bodies, as the two realised instantly, that yes, Quatesok maybe considering them (for the first time ever) as equals but so quickly after, the two also realised, this would come with even more pressure and urgency to deliver, more so, than when it was only Quatesok, alone, making decisions.

Later, when Quatesok was alone in his quarters, he questioned whether he should contact the Dime responsible for all this upset. Would they have any of the reasoning they had before they fell, though it was little even then from what Quatesok could remember? Was there a possibility that they still had the ability to realise the benefits of a better outcome for all?

Was a wipe or multiple wipes, wise of asking such a Dime, especially with his particular connection to such... this character?

Quatesok was becoming desperate, and he was needing outside of his logic, other rational thinkers, he was needing guidance, as he did not want this desperation that was building rapidly within him, to cause him to make any rash and permanently damaging decisions.

He longed at that moment, that someone, anybody would come to rescue and relieve the pressure within his mind...

"Do not think too hastily there," ...

Fearfully jumping from the shock of company!

"And DO NOT be angered nor discouraged by 'their' presence."

"How dare!" ...

"Now is not the time, Quatesok!"

Quatesok was enraged with the presence of the two...he was also more enraged that 'HE' himself, did not even sense, their decision to come to him.

"Already Quatesok, this is becoming a serious situation, and the possibilities of this ending badly will have dire, if not permanent detrimental consequences.

"The momentousness of it is having a significant effect upon your mind already, you are so distracted with it, you are forgetting to mind-out who surrounds you, not only is that dangerous but completely detrimental... to you and to... Rotherillia!"

The voice continued...

"Please I beg, take heed of my mind-ins to you, see why I shared, and then... see why 'they' are of tremendous use to you... to us."

The reason for Quatesok's unease, was that... Minkai had unexpectedly joined his company and she had done so also having the audacity to bring along... Risauma!

And still, this was not what was enraging Quatesok the most.

What he was so horrifyingly angered by, was that she had taken it upon herself to share with Risauma, his inner, most deepest kept secret.

Feeling betrayed and overwhelmingly vulnerable, Quatesok knew he had no choice but to believe Minkai's propose to sight her mind-ins, he would have to fully trust her and Risauma's allegiance to him, chancing them both possibly having the order of him sent to 'O' but as the mind-ins from Minkai entered his mind, he felt uncontrollable relief and yes, as the idea, thought (and Quatesok thought, so cleverly also) that Risauma had conjured for their approach to Obuseencentfinitus entered his mind, floods of objectives and added proposed approaches filled Quatesok's mind, suddenly between the three, multitudes of multiple ways and angles of how they would successfully, achieve and conclude this mission, came with ease and direction to their minds.

Finally.

"So, we agree, it should be me to orbit to O?"

"I'm still not completely comfortable with the settlement, are we sure we have covered all aspects for the visit?"

"I don't mean to press added tension to this situation, but I must stress, we are thin on time."

"Yes, you are right, this needs to be finalised."

"I know Quatesok you are in two minds and completely unsettled and unsure, but please believe, for once, my instinct... Risauma is the best suited for this mission."

"Yes, deep in my reasoning mind, I know you are right about this Minkai... Risauma, please do not take offence, I do not once doubt your ability, I know fully you are completely capable, understand, I do not want to put you in direct danger," Quatesok stressed.

All three during this meet, see them 'all' contradicting their original decisions...

"I am not offended Quatesok, you are right to deliberate, as you have stated previously, there is no space for mistakes and Quatesok... I know you are worried for my safety."

Risauma reassured.

"You are my best Seenhigh-Sypherer... you are my only Seenhigh-Sypherer, I have gone through many and you are the one, the 'only' one who meets my every expectational standards, with extraordinary qualities," Quatesok added.

Minkai pressed...

"It is up to you now, Quatesok. You now need to make contact with Obuseencentfinitus."

"Have them prepare my insight. I will be no more ready in the morning, then I am now... the sooner the better," Quatesok ordered.

"Yes Quatesok," Minkai dutifully, and swiftly replied.

Minkai summoned for an agent to call for the preparation and setting for the mind-in to O.

When everyone had cleared out of Quatesok's quarters, Minkai turned to him…

"Believe and believe more so than you confidently do with all else you feel strongly about.

Minkai paused breathily, then gave a reassuring glance of belief in her leader, continuing…

"as we Quatesok… have believed in you."

As Quatesok composed himself for his contact to O, he deepened into himself, memorising the reason for this visit, memorising their plan.

Once Quatesok had contacted O, they all agreed that no communication with the obvious Seenhigh-Sypherer… Liquylor, was to be made.

Risauma, cunningly and intelligently suggested another of O's Seenhighs. This was one of which in the past, had been reached out to and trusted and Risauma was confident they would have faith with the reason for the approach to O.

This was that…

A Dime at O was maybe being considered for reclaimant for redemption. This being a manipulated truth and one Risauma knowingly knew the Seenhigh being contacted for enlightenment there, would believe, as past encounters between the two of them, have had suggestive mind-ins, that such Dime 'should' be put forward for a pardoning for absolving.

The plan for the conclave was set.

"It is done Risauma. Your ally at O is ready to receive you."

"Why Minkai, are you seeing my departure?"

"Quatesok has confined himself to the temples, there he feels, he will be better equipped to deepen into his mind to strengthen yours whilst you are away. He fears greatly for your safe return and wants no interference from any, not even me! Until you do. "

"I will not fail him Minkai," Risauma reassured.

"Then come back Risauma, in one piece. That will be more gratifying to him and more so than the achievement of this mission," Minkai desperately insisted.

As Risauma parted from Rotherillia, the feeling inside, felt an instinct that knew...

this orbit to Obuseencentfinitus had to be the last of its kind.

When the highlight on O was made, Risauma felt a calm with lightening, and none, like ever, that had been felt before, it was reassuring, that finally, all could be turning for the better... for 'all'."

The greet.

"Ah there you are Risauma, in our bilious part of the region, you really do not want any to suspect."

"It has been a long time. How are you, Sashlia?" Risauma's aura language, spoke warmth and welcome all through it.

"My friend, I could be better, but this is O after all. Still at least one of us will be leaving these dregs."

The returning mind-in was also warm and inviting.

"Yes Sashlia, finally... Orellior will have justice," Risauma reassured.

"We have spoken so much of this moment Risauma, how did it come to be?"

"Quatesok has many connections, his findings of Orellior's good deeds, see a side of him turn gracious."

"Dare I ask of these findings."

"You know better than that, Sashlia."

Sashlia gave a subtle smile, then answered...

"That's all I need to know, Risauma. I'm convinced, Quatesok means no ill intent towards Orellior."

Sashlia was grateful for the Dime in question even being considered, that was enough for her.

The two spoke for some time, touching on subjects close to all within The Grid and beyond, beliefs and old concerns that had never past or left the minds of the combined and confinements of all Dimensions, both wondering, would there ever be peace...

"You know, Risauma, and I only mention this because I know of your loyalty with matters mentioned in confidence, and also, your understanding, to never to be repeated."

Risauma's posture sharpened upright instantly, with a direct interest, for what sounded very gripping and felt intriguingly relevant to the conversation shared by both.

Sashlia continued…

"Liquylor," she said, "I am deeply concerned about."

"Oh, but you are always concerned about the other Seenhighs here, and they of you, is that not part of your very survival within O?? Why now a greater concern or particularly for her?" Risauma was puzzled.

"Because dear friend her want to survive has begun to span a survival beyond Obuseencentfinitus,"

Sashlia stated in a serious tone.

Risauma questioned further…"What do you mean?? And forgive me when I say this, but your kind of Seenhigh are not meant, just not built to survive beyond O?!"

Sashlia continued…"And that is my problem Risauma, Liquylor has developed, strangely enough, an emotion, that enables her mind to want to strive passed the confinements of O, thus making it easier for others to follow, and this making me believe her newfound hunger for a different type of existence, was 'not' accumulated by mistake."

Risauma continued questioning…"Who do you think is party to her new abilities?"

"That, I do not know, but what I do know, is that they have definitely lost control of the agenda they planted in her mind, for wanting to leave O."

Grave concern ensued Risauma's face, questioning Sashlia further…

"So, what are you saying Sashlia, has Liquylor gone rogue?"

"That Risauma, is exactly my intuition, that, and the fact… she is also lightening others, with even sinister agendas here for the accomplishment of her escape."

"Others like who Sashlia?!" Risauma demanded.

"Others like Vilier, and we all know they're individual, scrupulous, heartless ways."

Risauma's expression showed that of demand that Sashlia reveal more, asking desperately…"What other Dimensions, Sashlia?"

Sashlia honestly did not have the answer Risauma was demanding, answering only as she could…

"Other Dimensions I cannot quite make out, lone rangers, I have …"

Suddenly.

"She!"

Risauma instantly filled with dread, as any (they had all been brainwashed amongst Rotherillia) connection linked to such a character, was always demanded to be treated with, zero tolerance and intent for immediate shut down of 'any' of her movements.

But as Sashlia went on further to explain, why she was so concerned for the encounters with Liquylor and 'She', it was unravelled and revealed a lightbulb moment within Risauma, the importance of 'Her'."

Risauma could not quite piece together the connections of Vilier, O, 'She' or other Mystery

Dimensions, but the realisation of the crucial and major link, engulfed and opened, what was beginning to look to be an enlightening vision.

As the visit to O nears to the end reader, it is realised...

"I may not be returning again Sashlia, this may be my last visit," Risauma assured.

"There is a comfort in that though, don't you think Risauma?" Sashlia returned the compliment.

"More than you can imagine," Risauma confidently answered.

The two minded-in the last of what would close, their requested, from their superiors, preferred, selected, information, settled in the deeper parts of their minds, that finally, hopefully, the path for all, would be clearer and better, for all to walk.

Risauma set to lighten back to home, but dread, again....She.

Risauma instinctively felt to mind-in a call for 'Her' wipe.

"Why???" Risauma deliberated.

Why the uncertainty, why the feeling, to save 'Her'?

This was not a coincidence, not by chance. 'She' was of more relevance than Risauma could understand.

"Not now Risauma, not yet," was the thought, passing the mind.

Jadelain sensed this. This was completely unusual, first Divinula and now Rotherillia, her mind instantly strengthened.

She must go on.

"Risauma, ready to lighten home."

Risauma felt an unease, was the decision in-mind, the correct one to make? Consultation was needed, but where? Who could be trusted?? A mutual mind was needed…

Minkai.

"Why have you called for this secret meeting, Risauma? I am confused, did all not go well at …?"

"Say no more Minkai, please just let me show you."

Risauma was desperate for Minkai's allegiance with the decision.

"Risauma, why?!! That was ludicrously idiotic, a complete risk on your life! But …"

Minkai composed herself.

"But I understand your reasoning, I see-think clear? For your choice."

"Why Minkai? Why is 'She' so important?" Risauma deliberated.

"I do not know Risauma, and I reluctantly also join you in your instinctive revelation. Quatesok must never learn of this, at least not for now, not until we, all of us, can completely justify and prove 'She' is of better use to 'all' within The Grid."

Minkai was known for her decisions based on heart-driven impulses, but even this was to test her intuition.

Belief.

Belief though, where all of this was concerned, was by no mistake, and driven by; she was driven, solely and most definitely wholly by her instinct.

Risauma needed to gather an explanation, suitable enough for Quatesok to deem reasonable to not strike. It needed to be convincing, that finally The Grid would need no more coaxing for the reins to be pulled on certain particulars.

"Tell me good news Risauma, worth 'your' risk for such a journey you have painstakingly taken."

This was demanded by one's leader with only an open for an answer that suggested success.

Risauma hesitated, holding all the mind-ability known to not reveal the obvious memorised information, damning to all, to oneself especially.

Compose was needed, then… the execution, within the delivery.

"Not now Quatesok, not yet. The information that is passing through other, through our Dimension alone 'will' cause the upset and uprise (enough to merit complete order, indefinitely) but at a cost."

Continuing with…

"You see Quatesok, there will be the controlled order, we all long for, but,"

Quatesok looked intensely, a painful stare, that knew the next sentence that followed, was 'not' going to be what he wanted to hear.

"'You' also Quatesok …"

Risauma continued...

"will be under intense scrutiny and will have truly little chance of becoming leader of any board voted for a 'one rule over all'."

Risauma had managed-was convincing enough to stall Quatesok.

More time had been bought.

Later, whilst all was calm, Minkai stood, staring over the lands of Rotherillia, she could feel the minds of her people, the unease, the undecided and those who were completely oblivious. Those were the ones she despaired for the most, the oblivious, they would be totally unawares, completely unprepared and ripped from the programming cushion they had been brainwashed and convinced would protect them.

As she glanced, her mind (not through choice) became distracted, as though something or someone, far away, wanted her attention.

Then realising...

"Hello Modyous," she minded back to the familiar encounter, one of the less menacing kinds.

"Minkai, how are you friend, looking into your mind (or what you are choosing to share) all is unsettled?"

"Yes Modyous, I am unsure, more and more of whom I can trust," she reluctantly answered.

Modyous pushed past this, stating..."I see you are aware of Villier."

Minkai paused, not too long as to be obvious, but enough to decide. She would keep this one close to her and Risauma.

"I know no more than what it is you show me Modyous."

She had to remain stern.

Modyous added…

"Ah Minkai, forever loyal to the one in hand, she is directly dealing with."

Minkai continued, though not denying the statement…

"More I'd say Modyous, I like to give the benefit of the doubt."

"Do you have doubts?" Modyous directly questioned.

Minkai immediately answered him, "More than ever before Modyous, but not what you so obviously believe, I think we both know, there is going to be an outcome that will shock the very core of this Grid."

And Modyous answered her in a tone agreeable to her understanding, "And Minkai, when it does, the one all question so profusely…

will be the one who saves us all."

"I must go Modyous," Minkai desperately stated.

"I sense you will 'not' be sharing our mind-in."

Modyous confidently asked, or rather stated, "No, not just yet."

Minkai reassured him.

"Is that wise?"

"It is necessary."

"Then as always Minkai, please be careful."

Minkai gave an answer next, that would most certainly reassure Modyous especially 'she' new the importance of what was at hand.

"Modyous, as long as my heart is driven by good, 'my' outcomes, I have learnt, will always be greater. Goodbye for now friend."

Tension was increasingly high within Rotherillia, their kind were all swiftly becoming aware of their Dictator's intentions to push his agenda of complete order of The Grid, and some were starting to panic, as this would bring the rest of the Dimensions to fuse together against them.

Not being as mindful as they would usually be, when communicating amongst one another, information was beginning to leak, a slackened practice was becoming a regular behaviour amidst the people, and general practice was starting to slip.

This was seeming to worsen, as Quatesok's paranoia blatantly became obvious and was growing ever stronger of the cohesion and manipulation he believed was taking place, forcing his mindset to push towards other Dimensions (The Grid itself) his persuasion of his obsessive belief of a dictatorship.

Those who usually sided with him, were starting to shadow away from him, as fear of the up-raw and heavy rise against him, was apparent and so obviously against him.

Dimensions across The Grid were starting to pressure The Grid for his annex, not only for their sake, but for the sake of Rotherillia themselves, as it was still not apparent who was the direct threat and Rother, it was feared, could make this easier for an enemy of The Grid to shut them all down in unison.

Despite all of this, Quatesok refused to stand down and stop his acts of aggression, ordered by The Grid.

Addressing his people…

"Rotherillia, it would seem we stand alone," …

The beginning of this sentence, the people of Rotherillia knew, was the start of their Dictator's once again, attempt to oppress 'all' within The Grid once more.

Seven: 7 Chapters In

"I've tried Modyous!" ...

Modyous so desperately knew he must evoke Jadelain's ability.

"Look within child, it is your birthright."

Jadelain deepened in, so consciously, that unconscious, it seemed she was.

She could hear, sense none around her...

Mimuluan.

Mimuluan was close, yet her actual person, was dimensions away.

Modyous, also far away.

Jadelain realising, and coming round...

"221811, you are needed at headquarters!"

Jadelain realised she was starting to long distance connect to Modyous and Mimuluan, without normal protocol to do so...

This was new.

The atmosphere was panicked, troubled by the intensity of concerning disorder and serious dilemma.

Zardinelle were under severe scrutiny, angst yet again from a familiar enemy...

Rotherillia.

Still with all that was occurring, Jadelian's thoughts were distracted, 'how'?? she was questioning, and how was she keeping this from every other high-ability Seenhigh-Sypherer across The Grid.

She needed to stay focused…

"Your thoughts 221811 need to be present."

Sharply, Jadelain switched to the matter, needing her attention.

She answered.

"We need the help of the indigenous kind of this land, we do not stand any chance of defeating mind-in battles, with any from Rother, if we do not use the old methods."

"What specifically were you in mind?"

This was asked of Jadelain by one of her senior superiors.

… "A perilous move!"

This answer came from one of Zardinelle's more quintessential leaders.

Arnolon.

"Ah, then what do you suggest Arnolon?"

Another senior asked.

"That Zardinelle use our signature strategy."

Arnolon replied.

Jadelain protested …

"Absolutely ridiculous Deniator! Rother will" …

She was instantly shut down by Deniator.

"Quiet 221811, I wasn't asking you, and so far, 'CHILD' you have brought us nothing but hardship anyway!"

"Rotherillia WILL crush us… we will be wiped."

Jadelain insisted.

"The 'child'." Arnolon answered with a slight low tone, under a half smile, also a small huff, followed by a tut. Suggesting maybe some truth in what she was saying…

"Maybe she is right," he finished…reluctantly.

"Are you saying we should listen to her??"

"I'm just saying Deniator, she might just have a point, we can't afford to take a chance with Rotherillia and Quatesok is more hell bound and blood thirsty than his usual self."

"What ancient method do you suggest 221811?" Deniator asked reluctantly.

"I suggest we speak to the 'Originals'." Jadelain replied solemnly, almost knowing this was to be rejected.

"And there it is again, I am not in favour of you again, have you lost your mind?!"

Deniator did not fail to let her down on her presumption of his reaction, he continued…

"Remember, they do not want some of us here either… you do remember 221811? That includes you especially."

"And remember Deniator, Rother will wipe them also, they have no choice," Jadelain spat.

"I will give it to her, Deniator, she has certainly learned our Zardilian ways."

"Shut up Arnolon, and prepare for her to go inland, up Halkain Mountain, and 221811 you will be going alone."

"With pleasure," Jadelain swiftly and confidently replied.

"221910," Jadelain called out, not looking over her shoulder, whilst acknowledging and still proceeding with gathering mind-ins from her composed, poised position.

"Why did you accept to go alone?" 221910 asked desperately.

"The simple answer... I do not trust you, 221910, the truthful answer ..."

Jadelain continued... "You are not ready, or more to the point, I am not ready to protect you."

"I'll go with the first, why do you keep underestimating yourself, 221811?...

Why Jadelain?" 221910 asked.

Jadelain turned to answer.

"That will not work 221910, and never put yourself at risk addressing me like that again."

"But you know ..."

221910 tried to continue, Jadelain cut her in her questioning.

"Whether you trust me or not 221910, keep in-mind Zardinelle and, in-mind... The Grid."

Jadelain sharply dismissed and returned to her duty for her commissioned agenda.

Time was passing, and all whilst trying to connect, no response. Why were they not responding?

She could find no reasoning with them, it seemed, even the reasoning of them also remaining was not enough to help...

Jadelain thought to herself... "The Minlactic Cluster, what if!?"

Then suddenly...

"Finally, you are not thinking of yourself."

Jadelain's body dropped, then as if her soul wrenched from her mind, she could see from the upper part of her head, the whole of Halkain Mountain.

"You did not think we would allow you here in person, did you?" The mind-in from an unknown, not revealing themselves, mocked her.

"You child would be the *last* to enter here... no, no, I'll better deal with you from afar."

"What was it that changed your minds?"

Jadelain was bewildered, what caused this enigmatic being to consider her?

"Your compassion child."

The voiced mind-answered, then continuing...

"Jadelain, you care, you do not know you care, you simply do not believe in yourself enough to believe in why you care."

Jadelain was puzzled, she quizzed further, she was troubled, but by what…

"Why is this so difficult for me?"

The voiced minding at that moment, shared with Jadelain. What would aid her?

"We will share with you child, the method that will help against Rotherillia. After that, you must do what you naturally know to do."

"How do I …?"

Jadelain's mind thought it was at a loss. She was not, she needed to believe.

The mind-in from the distant voice continued…

"Modyous is waiting Jadelain."

Ripped back to her original position, Jadelain shot up.

"221811 minding-in our method to hand."

"Well, well Deniator, it seems, she saves the day yet again."

Arnolon stated in that jubilant way he had about him.

Arnolon and Deniator, though shocked, were both relieved.

Deniator stood still in a stance, suggesting relief, but disbelief, confusion of how?? He did not know, but all the same, relief.

Jadelain prepared herself. Rother were going to attack, she and 221910 needed to be completely prepared. The old methods required practice, they were not easy to harness and when not used regularly, the strength of your mind, of your resistance, needed to be stern, quick and sharp with choosing decisions for your next mind-ins with greater outcomes, better for all.

She could feel.

Jadelain could sense Modyous, her intuition was getting stronger with connecting to him, she was realising also, she was more conscious.

She heard and felt Modyous…

"Yes Jadelain, just as Mimuluan had shown you, you remember, you must remember."

But it was difficult for her, with everyone around, the mind-ins that were taking place. 'Him' everything and everyone were somehow, trying to sypher her mind, but that was just it… they were trying, and she was beginning to be able to control it… control them.

"Concentrate."

Jadelain listened to Modyous, and with more ease than ever before.

Then as if with no effort, as though she always could… her mind began to flow, and as Modyous faded out, Jadelain realised…

No going back, she was on the right path.

"'They' must not be wiped." Her mind deeply revealed.

Eight: 8 Chapters In

"Rotherillia are minding to lighten here!" …

Starnyisia 'did not' want to get caught up in the conspiracy of the suspicion being aroused by Rother, they were confused as to why Rother wanted to visit them, were they not a Dimension, Rother preferred to stay on The Grid?? After all they were in favour of them when 'She' persuaded them to join? (She?)

Starnyisia began to panic, 'She' was the reason they were in question.

They knew they must separate themselves from her, they were glad they had previously rejected her requests to lighten… or so they thought?

Quatesok, back in Rotherillia was becoming more unnerved and extremely demanding, he summoned his confidant…

"Minkai… immediately, come now!"

"What Quatesok, would you like me to do?"

"Something is not right Minkai, something is being kept from us, from me."

"What is it that you feel?"

Minkai was more concentrated than ever.

Quatesok shot a look at her and for a moment, Minkai felt a panic.

"He knows!" she thought to herself.

Quatesok glared a long stare, Minkai waited intensely.

"Prepare a visit to Starnyisia," he ordered.

Minkai was confused further.

"Why?" she asked, trying not to reveal.

Quatesok continued in his demanding rant...

"They have been too quiet," he blurted angrily matter-of-fact.

Minkai attempted to answer him...

"But they are peaceful peo ..."

"Prepare a visit!" Quatesok demandingly spat.

"As you command."

Minkai let out a huge sigh when she left his quarters. He did not suspect her, but it was becoming overwhelmingly harder to sypher out the piece of information only she and Risauma possessed.

Meanwhile in strained, stressed Starnyisia...

"Minkai will be coming here, Tarklimar."

"Good, it means Quatesok is unsure of us. Make sure you make her very welcome, make sure she has nothing to suspect us of."

Starnyisia, set a lightening to their Dimension, grand and to the richest land within their world. They displayed an embrace so warm, that only acceptance of her coming, Minkai could read from it.

Minkai did suspect, but not because she suspected them, no, because within this meet, its outlandish over-elaborated play-out, was a great cover and made it easier for other underhand dealings to take place.

"Who else was there?!" Minkai desperately, critically wondered.

"A great show Ampmal, tell me though, how do you keep up with those who are not supposed to be here?"

No holds barred was Minkai, when she delivered this statement.

Ampmal looked shockingly frightful, but knew he had to win Minkai back.

He answered instantly, fear in his throat, hoping for her approval.

"I, I can reassure you Minkai, there's none here, not supposed to be here."

Minkai looked at him pitifully as though to show she felt sorry for his unwanted put-upon-him sudden pressure, and so unexpectedly too.

"At least say it convincingly, Ampmal," Minkai answered jestingly.

Ampmal sighed relieved, but not impressed by her taunting, stating…

"Please don't tease Minkai, there's enough pressure without you making mockeries of this situation."

Then looking confusingly at her and asking in a high tone…

"Why is Quatesok so paranoid, Minkai? It makes the rest of us very nervous you know."

Minkai answered in a way that showed even she was confused and at a loss, as to why her leader was choosing to take such a drastic stance.

"Oh, I don't know Ampmal, but any excuse to be out of harm's way or reach of him, is enough for me to make myself scarce."

The two shared a quiet giggle, more serious matters were about to start and the two knew, it was few and far between for moments of slight joy.

As the welcome celebrations neared to an end, Minkai and her entourage were taken to the Official Assembly Rooms.

"Minkai, so long we have not seen each other, how long now?"

A familiar voice, but one hiding an undertone.

"What is the mind-in being kept from me Tarklimar? And quick, Quatesok will suspect."

The voice quickly answered, upset or reasons to suspect were not wise right now.

"It is nothing Minkai, I can assure you, Villier have passed through, the people of this land don't want to upset Quatesok, you understand."

"I do…Quatesok but The Grid may not. Why would you not declare that??"

Minkai demanded answers… fast.

Tarklimar dutifully answered,

"I simply had no answer for when they would require a reason for them being here, something (or one) spooked and scared them away before I could get any information as to why they were here.

"They had already begun to sypher us all out, before we could mind their reason for being here. Imagine us trying to explain that to Quatesok alone, *and then* The Grid, that would not have fared well, as well you know, Minkai. Please have a little compassion."

Minkai reassured, "Your explanation is fitting, but now we have two problems."

"Oh??" Tarklimar questioned.

"Yes," Minkai answered immediately and direct.

"What??"

Minkai looked up at Tarklimar, straight into his eyes with concern, she answered…

"Firstly, who is or was here to frighten them away, and biggest of all…

why and where are Villier going next?"

Tarklimar took this opportunity to ask for Rother to extend their visit.

"Minkai, would you stay? Your Seenhigh's are much more advanced than ours, the threat may still be here, and besides, there is a big banquet later."

Minkai accepted.

"Yes Tarklimar, we will stay."

Tarklimar, instantly became relieved, excitedly stating…

"Good! we will prepare the Bathownria Quarters for you."

Minkai looked satisfyingly shocked at Tarklimar, as these were lavish chambers, only saved for eminent visitors to the Starnyisian Dimension.

"Yes," Tarklimar exclaimed to Minkai's silent satisfied expression upon her face. He continued…

"It would be a delight for us to have you stay there."

The feast that evening was true to form, just as grand as the welcoming festival. Minkai and her Troop, although enjoying all that was taking place, still concentrated on mind-ins, suggesting any fret.

As time was nearing to leave, nothing came to light of any great concern, Minkai was finishing with the mind-in to lighten home…

'She', Minkai thought.

Minkai was strangely aware of 'her', but not so knowingly why?? She did not understand this.

"What should I do?" Minkai thought again.

She knew she should mind-in, but something was bidding her not to.

She wouldn't this time. Minkai decided not to call in.

Instead decided to stay within Starnyisia, there must be a way to enquire, without revealing.

It would seem though, that Starnyisia were not so successful from keeping Villier's visit as they thought, as another would make contact with them…

"And you are sure that they have definitely made contact with Starnyisia?"

"Most certainly."

"Why would they not reveal, their kind are honest usually??"

"What course of action would you like to take?"

"Set a mind-in, we will deal as always, we are not irrational."

"Yes, Modyous."

"Thank you, Eathinua."

What Modyous was not aware of, was that others were frequenting also, in the lands of the Starnyisian Dimension.

This was not Modyous' concern though, he was aware that other Dimensions may have caught wind of the information he was also enquiring about.

Intelligence was never scarce amongst the more advanced Dimensions.

Although Minkai could sense Jadelain, she wasn't quite sure she was present. This confused her greatly, normally it was easier to know there was another, and especially if one was so close.

Jadelain, with her abilities growing stronger, knew most certainly Rother were here in Starnyisia, but whilst having the ability to sypher them out of knowing she was there too, she did not yet have the ability to sypher why they were.

Instead, she would dangerously move amongst the people, maybe they had the answers, but who was trustworthy, more loyal to Rother, this was seemingly more strenuous on her mind than ever before.

There was the one group Jadelain recalled that were the most peaceful amongst the Starnyisians, were less politically driven, more, she remembered, driven by their soul and spirit.

She would go to the region she remembered last, hoping they still remained. As she steadied the crowds, minds amidst them violently, desperately, tried the intrusive syphering of her mind.

She knew she must not reveal to all, her identity.

Help did move within the groups she quickly realised, the skill theirs and her mind had to adapt, minding-in the place of the peaceful kind to her, whilst both she and them, had to block out the intrusive syphering mind-ins.

Different paths and false leads had to be given to the opposing rival adversary, like a diversion division with every competitive physical, played out through a mental battle instead.

Through all this Jadelain was hearing the whispers, whispers of Rother, whispers of...

Villier.

Finally, she would reach.

"No worries Jadelain, they will not sypher here."

"Ankniera," Jadelain called, as she fell to her knees, exhausted, and almost beat.

"Quick, go fetch her," Ankniera commanded.

Hours would pass before Jadelain came around again, but safe now she was under the protection of Ankniera and her group.

As Jadelain began to wake, a pressured sound so raucous and blindingly disturbing, rushed her brain. She desperately held tight in her mind, the urge this was causing her to reveal all she knew, with this a connection, although breath bound her to all Dimensions, then... gone.

She shot straight up, just as before, in Zardinelle, but the connection and memory of this, just-moments-ago experience, instantly passed.

"But what?... How??" Jadelain thought.

Another mind-in...

"Come over, Jadelain."

Ankniera.

"So, Rother have caught wind of dishonourable behaviour too, then?" Jadelain queried.

"It would seem so Jadelain ..."

The two sat, discussing, at times, debating, deliberating, other times agreeing, jesting, gesturing what move each one should possibly make next. The night moved fast on a slow clock, winding, whilst outside, Ankniera's group minded-steadily-out, the threat of Rother, the threat that seemingly moved amongst their own, this was Jadelain's biggest concern of all.

"I despair desperately, Ankniera," Jadelain confessed.

"You feel it too, Jadelain."

"Ankniera also."

"Your people along with Villier and Rotherillia, are also menacing,"

Jadelain continued.

"I agree, Jadelain."

Ankniera agreed.

Jadelain continued further...

"Almost a hex, a curse, their divided opinions are a danger, this is troubling, and I feel could jeopardise and impact, stopping a greater outcome for The Grid."

A short silence cloaked the atmosphere around the two, then, on into the late night their conversation continued.

Jadelain would move on through early morning, knowing now of Rother, but no further forward of Villier.

Rother were aware of 'Her' but what started as a fret felt from her, soon turned to an admiration.

Jadelain, they were strangely noticing, was not posing a fret with this newfound ability she had acquired. Yes, they were not familiar with it, but she showed no signs she would use it in any way in a threatening manner.

They were not sure of her intentions, but were sure, they felt an unusual ease.

Minkai especially was not intimidated by her, and though this was understood amongst their troops, they silently knew they must never again speak of it. They were 'all' in unison prepared to ignore, blindsight their selves of her presence.

Clearer still, was her path, her visions more vivid, almost known, of how she must proceed.

Finally... 'Him' again.

She had been waiting for this, had been apprehensive for its coming.

He instantly let her know, that she was moving instinctively, she was surely on the right road, the right way.

"Carry on, Jadelain," she told herself, "carry on."

Modyous, wasn't far behind as Jadelain and Rotherillia left Starnyisia.

"I take it I will be no further able to retain Villier's doings, none more than Rother nor Jadelain?"

"So sorry, Modyous," Tarklimar exclaimed.

"No, all is good here Tarklimar, I sense we may all be on the right path anyway."

Nine: 9 Chapters In

Genvia is on her way...

Uliminous seldom had visitors, and seldom accepted them, Genvia was one of their preferred.

This was purely because of her angelic calm persona.

Genvia infectiously brought purity and peace wherever she attended, and if frequenting your Dimension, she only believed you were of the same interior and exterior as her own and worth her presence.

Although, this particular visit to Uliminous, was one, for an unusual request...

"Why Genvia, to what honour do we owe your person here this present time?"

"My instincts tell me you already know why I came."

"Maybe dearest, but to hear it would be more fitting."

"Amulieion, I know you sensed my premonitions already, but 'I' still know not, what I am to do with them" ...

Genvia was seeking the mystical powers of Uliminous, their ability of persuasion and illusion.

Was she right to rely on them, for what she so greatly needed reassurance?

Back in Obuseencentfinitus...

"So, as you see Liquylor, 'She' is of particularly good use indeed, you agree?"

The tone of this slithering little snake alone, let alone his grilling, high-pitched eery screech, irritated Liquylor...

"Quiet," she demanded.

Tinnateenum instantly bawled and creeped backwards, slowly, cowardly.

"Have these useless miscreant creations, something useful for a change Liquylor, or was it a complete waste of time, their existence on The Grid or ever?" Highest exclaimed, with a sighing, exhausted expression.

"They seem to have information on 'She' ..."

Wodenine.

"Wodenine joined The Grid when Globelious was on our board, his affairs and procedures were already under question and so underhandedly deceitful, devious, with contempt and venomous intent, towards 'all' within the entire Minlactic Cluster.

"Not one, did he favour, and all he despised. He convinced our board and then The Grid, Wodenine would be of use, he persuaded them, as soldiers, their hunger to please would drive them to sacrifice themselves in mind-in battles.

The Grid did not buy this at first, but his cunningness, stated, strength in numbers...I always knew what he was, but his high status was hard in breaking or making them realise what was the character with which they were really dealing.

His vengeance towards all and especially 'us' grew an evil that could only mean one thing...

'O'..." Amulieion finished.

"Yes ..." Genvia ended.

"And now I understand Genvia, but do you?"

"I do, but I don't Amulieion, that is why I am driven here, I think? Help me please!"

"What does your heart tell you or not?"

"Both," Genvia exclaimed.

"Can you do both?" Amulieion questioned her further.

"Hide! Is what is in mind."

"A temporary solution, maybe?" Amulieion whispered questioningly to her.

"Do you choose hide?" he persuasively asked her further.

"Your choice of course, Genvia," he added swiftly, subtly after.

"Hide," Genvia exclaimed.

"Then hide it is," he promptly answered her.

Genvia left Uliminous, feeling as though they helped, but also feeling confused with how...

This was the mystery and mastery of Uliminous.

Ten:10 Chapters In

"Who else knows of this Tinnateenum?" Liquylor insisted.

"No one!" Tinnateenum slithered.

"Why do I feel that's a lie, nevertheless you've done well."

Liquylor was not convinced, but she was limited, bound tighter than usual with her flexibility she would normally have in choosing the right information for a greater gain, her greater gain.

Time was running out; she would reluctantly have to accept this slithering creature's word.

"Thank you," leaving quickly and slivering back as fast they could, Wodenine had managed, yet again to remain in Highest's consideration 'not' for wipe."

"A useful piece for our agenda, Highest?" Liquylor strategically suggested.

"A perfect find Liquylor, your upgrades are certainly paying their costs ..."

Highest was pleased yet again.

This was always a win for Liquylor as long as he remained in favour of her.

But whilst Highest and Liquylor were meddling with the safety of The Grid, others were determined to save it, others like Rotherillia.

"Why Uliminous, Quatesok?"

"They always know everything Minkai, I am sure of it."

Quatesok felt he was closing in.

"But we always have so many obstacles when seeking anything from this kind, your frustrations with them alone, aggravate you terribly."

Minkai desperately tried to convince him otherwise.

"Minkai!"

Quatesok angrily (and frustratingly with Minkai) continued...

"I 'will' find a solution or the cause to all that is occurring here, and I will be successful for my 'one united order'. It is imperative for everyone that I convince The Grid finally of this, for the last time ..."

Continuing he demanded...

"Now, prepare, they are usually more pliable when I send you."

Although Minkai was tiring of the lightenings to other Dimensions, she was grateful for the piece, Quatesok was becoming unbearable, and it seemed this time around, more than ever before.

"Will he be sending me, Minkai?"

"Do not worry Risauma, he will never mistakenly resist sending you, his most dependable Seenhigh...So yes, you will be relieved from him also."

The two knew to mind this to each other, deep enough so Quatesok did not suspect.

Anything of late, erupted an outrage from him, and his decision making was unpredictable and unacceptably irrational.

Never-the-less, they were both going and needed to deliver.

The contact made to Uliminous, already was showing this was not going to be an easy feat.

Minkai threat, for whether there would be an acceptance for a lightening there at all.

"They are not enthusiastic for our wanting to come, Minkai." An agent of the lightening functions stressed.

"Send me in Risauma," Minkai demanded.

Minkai intended to share with Uliminous but knew this could be costly.

"You're sending for me Minkai, but you are already minding-in to me."

"Yes Risauma, I do not want any other to suspect."

"Do you think it is wise to share this information with Uliminous, Minkai?"

"It is our only hope of getting them to accept our lightening there."

"Then I Minkai, will do the mind-in, I will be able to sypher it to them, that best suits their intentions."

The information Risauma had for Uliminous 'did' suit for their interest to accept Rother, but Rother knew, this journey was not going to be easy.

Uliminous responded that illuminating, riddlesome way, only they could…

"Miss Minkai, do we honour, or owe your visit?... Never mind... telling, will be in time, or on time, I seldom remember, do you child?"

Already the games began, Minkai shot her answer back, letting her opposite party know she was in no mood.

"Not now, Amulieion, I haven't the time," Minkai desperately demanded.

"Yes, as I remember, you 'do' ... not nor try too either. Perfectly delivered Minkai, just as said."

More riddles from Amulieion, but what did she expect?

She demanded...

"Amulieion, you can see we are here on a peaceful visit, what we or 'I' have shared with you, surely confirms that for you?"

"Yes, you have confirmed," confidently answered by Amulieion.

"Then you do have knowledge of what is accruing within The Grid?"

Minkai was breathily hopeful.

"Yes Minkai, you confirmed that."

Minkai looked confused.

"What do you mean?" she asked frustratingly.

"Why, your information dear...confirms everything."

Amulieion, playfully confident, yet again.

"I shared that with you, Amulieion."

Minkai was growing tired.

"Of course, you did, Miss Minkai, and for that The Grid is extremely grateful."

Minkai was beginning to tire, her mission here, was no further in completing. How could she return to Quatesok, empty minded?

Then suddenly, almost by mistake, Minkai visioned 'Her' …

"What with Jadelain Amulieion?" she asked instantly.

"Well now Minkai, you do press mind-in selective-sighting…but I'm afraid, you're not ready yet."

Minkai felt her mind separate… her people, then fading…Jadelain, suddenly gone…Quatesok.. "He would be furious" … more separation, her mind was splitting, she was forgetting, her kind, they were forgetting, 'all'? she thought, "Why all of us?!" she asked desperately.

Then…

"Not all of you."

She turned in her mind.

Amulieion.

"Just those of you that are here…Sorry Minkai, time for you all to go home."

Then as if the lightening to Uliminous had never happened.

Back…

Back they all were at Rotherillia.

Uliminous rarely used this method, the risks alone could cost a Dimension, a form of limbo… permanently.

"This must not be done again, Amulieion."

"Then, 'my mind'," Amulieion referred to himself ...

"You must never invite them here again."

Back at Rotherillia, Quatesok was not happy, furious in fact.

"Quatesok, Sir, it was not our fault, you must understand?!"

"Yes!!" Quatesok bellowed.

"I understand you all failed me!" he continued.

He demanded they leave his presence immediately.

"I will deal with them all later, Uliminous 'Amulieion', liars, deceivers, when I set this straight with The Grid, the great conglomerate we stand upon...

Glacoure... will be free of these kinds, these fiends forever."

He deliberated in his mind. His frustrations ensuing.

When Quatesok finally calmed with his discomfort and frankly, frustration, that yet again, he could not bend nor defeat the power, known of Uliminous, though mysterious, still unable for any to decipher or control, this troubled Quatesok, another seed began to fester within his mind. Minding-in to Minkai...

"Minkai, am I wrong for trying?"

Minkai attempted to reassure him.

"Quatesok, no one individual here, on Rotherillia, thinks that you are wrong."

"But?" Quatesok gestured for her to continue (almost knowing the answer).

"But," she continued...

"The others within The Grid find your agenda extreme."

Quatesok instantly took offence.

"I 'will' prove these Dimensions unruly, I will prove, Uliminous is one of them.

That is all Minkai, this mind-in is over."

Quatesok allowed the niggling in his mind to continue, turning to a pondering in his brain.

Over and over, he thought…

"Why are Uliminous here, a part of The Grid, they are not worthy!?" His mind spat.

"An unruly kind." Again, over and over (in his mind)

"Mocking me of paranoia, THEY are my paranoia, them and others." In the depths of his mind and thinking deeper still, infuriating his mind further, he thought…

"Uliminous never directly involve themselves with The Grid, if it were up to me, 'I' would eliminate them from The Grid," he thought.

"From the security of The Grid," he went on.

"I would have them wiped."

Then mentally torturing himself further, Quatesok thought of Uliminous' response, Amulieion's response, hearing it clearly in his mind…

"Well now, that's just a matter of opinion Quatesok, isn't it…isn't it???"

"Minkai!!!" Quatesok bellowed again.

Eleven: Final Chapter In

"So maybe Said's were right."

"Don't speak too soon."

"Oh ..."

"They do not know yet."

"Ah yes...

This bit must complete."

"Yes, that's right mind 'She' must know ..."

A conversation Amulieion and his mind have all the time.

Did Sierephiar have to go? Will the other Dimensions, The Minlactic Cluster remain?

Time direction will tell.

Jadelain was starting to trace her steps, Divinula, Rotherillia 'why'?" she thought to herself, "what was it?" she was thinking, 'She' was missing.

Her intuition spurred her further forward.

Back before...

"Yes ..." Genvia ended.

"And now I understand Genvia, but do you?"

"Hide! Is what is in mind."

"Do you choose hide?" Amulieion persuasively asked her further.

"Hide!" Genvia exclaimed.

"Then hide it is," Amulieion promptly answered her.

Uliminous... good with subtle manipulation.

All of which pieced 'Her' path.

As Jadelain leaves Starnyisia, leaves Ankniera, she knows instantly, she must find Vilier, find... Kinlye.

"Where?" her mind intensively questions. "Where would they go??

Obuseencentfinitus!" Her instincts heighten greatly.

She demands a lightening there instantly.

"221910 'O' immediately!"

"But why 22 ..."

"Just do it!!"

221910 rushes for the lightening of Jadelain to 'O' then concentrating like never before, the pressure building in her brain, as fast as her mind could piece the path, a speed never done before with the visual of it, she minds to Jadelain an instant sighting of Obuseencentfinitus.

As soon as Jadelain materialises there, her feet barely touching, she moves at a pace, never achieved before...

"Kinlye!" she screams.

Kinlye drops to his knees, Jadelain's abilities heighten, she freezes Kinlye's mind, he becomes embolised.

Jadelain syphers from his brain, Kinlye is powerless to her ability, then Jadelain learns.

From Kinlye's mind, Jadelain visualises her true kind, her birthright... her true abilities.

"This was the true path I was to walk," she realises.

These were all a reset.

Then flooding into her brain, all the paths she had walked before, the reasons she kept resetting, then finally she learns the biggest change... Sierephiar!

She could never wipe them before; she just did not have the heart.

This was the reason she had always failed before.

Her kind had sent her there to The Grid, it was her lesson, they had wiped her memory of them. You see The Grid needed to learn unity but Jadelain's lesson was sacrifice. When back home, she sympathised with The Grid and her ancestors banished her to The Grid to learn, not all who necessarily think individually, think right. If she could sacrifice Sierephiar, she would learn, not all can be saved, The Grid's separation from The Minlactic Cluster, may have seemed to them, a worthy choice (after all, they were just trying to save themselves?) but in the long run, they lived in a constant reset, simply because they did not believe in the protection from the unity of The Cluster.

Then it all began to make sense, her kind before taking her to Zardinelle, making contact with Uliminous, they instruct that Uliminous must persuade

Genvia to hide Sierephiar, but Genvia must do this with her own heart, otherwise it would not work.

This is why Genvia desperately convinces Jadelain to wipe.

Jadelain learns, it is Genvia's voice she hears in Sierephiar.

Jadelain knows instinctively who her next target is.

Globelious.

"So, you still come for me Jadelain, is there no place in your heart for me?"

Jadelain does not hesitate, melting the mind of Globelious, she realises, this should have been the act Sierephiar chose when they had the chance - once rogue, always rogue.

Her next target... Liquylor.

This would be no easy feat.

She knew Liquylor had hidden her mind.

Suddenly everyone that Jadelain had connected with, appeared...

"They are the guilty ones."

Jadelain knew that just because she could hear their individual voices, Liquylor was controlling the diction, making them all (Liquylor) repeat their disappointment with Jadelain, her insecurities, her failures over and over again.

Jadelain began to weaken.

"Find yourself Jadelain," she told herself.

She strengthened.

Then Liquylor showed Jadelain her own kind.

"They didn't want you Jadelain."

Then repeated by the visual of them...

"We didn't want you Jadelain...YOU'RE A DISAPPOINTMENT."

Jadelain fell to the ground.

"That's right Jadelain," Liquylor continued.

"You were a disappointment, do you remember? Do you remember, Jadelain?"

Weaker still Jadelain became.

Then...

"Strength, strength, strength," whispered in her head. For the first time, Jadelain was listening to her own voice, but now she heard nothing but positivity.

Stronger she was becoming, clearer in her mind.

No Liquylor, you are the disappointment.

Then within an instant, Liquylor's functions, ground to a halt, no more was she a fret, to Jadelain, The Grid and most of all, The Minlactic Cluster.

Jadelain had learned, that separate feelings of superiority were, in some cases, detrimental, sometimes a one-mind-unite is what we all need... to save all.

Him.

"I didn't lose you?"

He answers Jadelain, thankful, that finally he can reveal his identity...

"No child, you never have."

Land of Alterium ...

"You've got that same look on your face."

"I know...

She made it."

The End...

For Now.